Meet the staff of
THE TREEHOUSE TIMES

AMY—The neighborhood newspaper is Amy's most brilliant idea ever—a perfect project for her and her friends, with a perfect office location—the treehouse in Amy's backyard!

ERIN—A great athlete despite her tiny size, Erin will be a natural when it comes to covering any sports-related story in the town of Kirkridge.

LEAH—Tall and thin with long, dark hair and blue eyes, Leah is the artistic-type. She hates drawing attention to herself, but with her fashion-model looks, it's impossible not to.

ROBIN—With her bright red hair, freckles and green eyes, and a loud chirpy voice, nobody can miss Robin—and Robin misses nothing when it comes to getting a good story.

Keep Your Nose in the News with
THE TREEHOUSE TIMES Series
by Page McBrier

(#1) UNDER 12 NOT ALLOWED
(#2) THE KICKBALL CRISIS

Coming Soon

(#4) FIRST COURSE: TROUBLE
(#5) DAPHNE TAKES CHARGE

PAGE McBRIER grew up in Indianapolis, Indiana, and St. Louis, Missouri, in a large family with lots of pets. In college she studied children's theater and later taught drama in California and New York. She currently lives in Rowayton, Connecticut, with her husband, Peter Morrison, a film producer, and their two small sons.

THE TREEHOUSE TIMES #3

Spaghetti Breath

Page McBrier

AN AVON CAMELOT BOOK

THE TREEHOUSE TIMES #3: SPAGHETTI BREATH is an original publication of Avon Books. This work has never before appeared in book form.

AVON BOOKS
A division of
The Hearst Corporation
105 Madison Avenue
New York, New York 10016

First Avon Camelot Printing: December 1989

For Art Klein,
who set me on the path

Chapter One

"So who did you get?"

Amy Evans reached into her pocket for the neatly typed name her teacher Mr. Eric had given her. "Stella Moss," she announced. She studied the slip of paper. "She lives in those apartments on Polk Street. Do you know her?"

Amy's best friend, Erin Valdez, covered her mouth and giggled.

"Do you, Erin?" repeated Robin Ryan, who was walking beside them.

Erin nodded.

"Well . . . is she nice?" asked Amy.

Erin giggled again. "Her breath smells like spaghetti."

"How would you know?" said Robin.

"She was on my paper route," said Erin. "Why? Who do *you* have?"

1

Robin cringed. "Bert and Wanda some-body."

Erin and Amy burst out laughing.

"*Bert* and *Wanda?*" said Erin, holding her sides. "What kind of names are those?"

February was Adopt-a-Grandparent Month at Kirkridge Middle School, and for one after-noon a week each student was supposed to spend time with his or her "adopted" grand-parent. Amy, who was in the sixth grade, thought it sounded like it could be fun. Maybe they could even write about their "grandpar-ents" in the *Treehouse Times.*

The *Treehouse Times* was Amy, Robin, and Erin's neighborhood newspaper. Leah Fox worked on the newspaper too, but she didn't go to Kirkridge Middle School. Instead, she went to a private school called the Day School.

"Well, *I* have Margaret Donaldson," an-nounced Erin. "I think she's that lady with the silvery hair who jogs past our house every morning."

"Figures," said Robin with a sigh. "You get the jock. I get Bert and Wanda." She stopped long enough to retie her left sneaker. "I won-der if Mr. Eric planned that?"

"What else do you know about Mrs. Moss?" Amy asked Erin, ignoring Robin's usual com-plaining.

Erin shrugged. "Nothing much. She's sort of skinny and old."

"They're all old," said Robin. "They're grandparents."

"My grandmother isn't old," said Amy. "She has blonde hair like all the Hotchkisses." Amy resembled the Hotchkiss side of her family. Blonde hair, green eyes, glasses. All Hotchkisses wore glasses.

"My grandmother Remedios has blonde hair, too," said Erin, who was Mexican-American. "She dyes it."

The three girls laughed and turned into Amy's driveway. Ever since third grade they'd been spending almost every afternoon after school together. That's what made their new neighborhood newspaper so much fun. "I wonder if Leah's home yet," said Amy, pushing open the kitchen door. In the good weather, the girls usually met in Amy's backyard in her treehouse where they had their newspaper office. Now that it was cold outside, they'd moved into Amy's kitchen.

Robin walked over to the refrigerator and helped herself to a diet soda. Robin was a tiny bit plump, with red hair and freckles. "Maybe we should make the February issue a Valentine's issue," she said.

"Or President's Day," said Amy.

"Or Black History Month," said Erin.

"Or Groundhog Day," said Robin. She cupped her hands together under her chin and

3

chomped her teeth together, which made them all crack up.

"Hi, guys," said Leah, pushing open the door. She handed Amy her mail and then unwrapped herself from a long black scarf-and-hood thing. Leah was sort of exotic. She had long dark hair and was tall and thin like a model. She always wore black.

"Thanks," said Amy. She noticed an envelope addressed to her on the top of the pile. "What's this?" She tore it open.

"A valentine!" said Robin. "Who's it from?"

Amy turned the card over. It was a big store-bought card with a heart on the outside. Inside it said, "Have a Happy Valentine's Day." It was signed, "From Your Secret Friend."

"Maybe it's from a boy," said Robin.

Amy blushed and then checked the envelope for the postmark. "St. Louis."

"So it could be a boy," said Robin. "It could be anyone in our class." Kirkridge was a suburb of St. Louis.

"I wish someone would send me a valentine," said Erin. She'd had a crush on Robin's cousin Matt O'Connor for a couple of months now.

"It's probably from my grandmother," said Amy. She looked inside the envelope for a check.

"Amy got a valentine," sang Robin. "I'm going to put it in my gossip column."

4

"Robin! Don't!" said Amy. "I told you. It's probably from my grandmother." Robin had the biggest mouth in town. "We got our Adopt-a-Grandparents today," Amy said to Leah, hoping to change the subject. She told Leah about Mrs. Moss.

"Maybe that's who sent the valentine," said Robin.

"Would you stop it?" said Amy. "I haven't even met her yet."

"Shouldn't we be working on the paper right now?" said Erin, coming to the rescue.

Amy grabbed a pencil and a sheet of paper. "What do we want to write about?" She glared at Robin. *"Besides* valentines?"

Every month the paper reported on news around the neighborhood. Some of the regular features were "Neighbor of the Month," "What's Happening," editorials, and "Letters to the Editor," if they got any. Because the newspaper had been Amy's idea, she was the editor, which meant she had the final say. Robin and Erin were the feature and investigative reporters. Leah was the art director and photographer. It usually worked out pretty well.

"I have an idea," said Leah. "Instead of Erin writing her 'Neighbor of the Month,' you should all write about your adopt-a-grandparents. I can take their pictures."

"That's a great idea!" said Amy, jotting it

down. "I was hoping we could do something like that. Do you mind, Erin?"

Erin shook her head.

"What else?" said Amy.

No one said anything.

"What if we try going door-to-door, to see if anyone has any news for us?" said Amy.

"To eight thousand people?" said Robin.

Amy made a face. "I meant our immediate neighborhood."

Erin jumped out of her chair. "Let's go now!"

"Right now?" said Robin. "It's freezing."

But Erin was already putting on her ski parka. "It's boring sitting around. I hate winter." Erin came from California where it never got cold. "Are you coming?"

"Why not?" said Amy, throwing on her coat. She tucked her reporter's notebook into her pocket.

"Wait for me," said Robin. "I don't want to miss anything."

Amy grinned. "What are you waiting for, then?"

They started up Washington Street, Amy's block. "Let's try that new family that just moved in," said Erin, the bravest.

"Which family?" Amy asked.

Erin pointed to a yellow house with brown shutters. "That one. Mom said they're from Illinois."

They all ran up the steps and huddled around after ringing the door bell. A young woman holding a baby came to the door. "Yes?"

"We're from the *Treehouse Times*," said Erin, "your friendly neighborhood newspaper."

The woman nodded.

"Do you have any news?" asked Erin.

"News?" said the woman. She switched the baby to her other hip.

"Anything exciting happen to you lately?" said Robin. "Besides moving, of course?"

"Not really," said the woman. The baby started to fuss. "Do any of you baby-sit?"

"When I turn twelve I can," said Amy. The baby spit up all over its mother's sweater. "I won't be twelve for a while, though," she added.

"Well, sorry I can't help you," said the woman.

"That's okay," said Erin.

At the next house, a woman named Mrs. Tilly told them that her dog had just died. "Maybe you can write up a little tribute to him," she said. "His name was Patches."

"I used to see you walking him," said Amy politely. "He was short and—"

"Fat." The woman chuckled, finishing her sentence. "Charlie fed him too many dog biscuits."

Amy nodded. "We'll try to find room to mention him."

As they walked away from the house, Robin said, "Are we really going to write a tribute to a dog?"

Amy shrugged. "Maybe." Amy hated to hurt people's feelings, which was sometimes a good thing and sometimes a bad thing. It was good because she cared about people, which was important if you were going to write a newspaper. It was bad because it sometimes made it hard to be objective. They turned up the next street.

"Hey," said Erin to Robin. "Isn't this where your adopt-a-people live?"

"Hayes Avenue," said Robin. "I guess it is."

A mischievous smile crossed Erin's face. "Let's go introduce ourselves," she said. "What number?"

Robin fished a wrinkled piece of paper out of her pocket. "Thirty-two fourteen."

"Over there," pointed Leah. "The turquoise house with the Astro-turf in front." She started to laugh.

"What's so funny?" said Robin.

"Nothing," said Leah. "I never noticed the house before." Under her breath she added, "I don't know *why.*"

They all trudged across the street and stood in front of the matching turquoise mailbox. "Moscowitz," it read.

Robin scowled.

"What's wrong?" said Amy.

"You guys are making fun of my grandparents."

"No, we're not," said Amy. "Come on. Let's go say hello. If you want, we can go meet mine next." This time Amy led the way and rang the bell.

A short, heavyset, bald man wearing leather slippers answered the door. "Yes?"

"Hi," said Amy. "I'm Amy Evans and this is Robin Ryan, your new adopt-a-grandkid." She pulled Robin forward.

"Who is it, Bertie?" called a woman from the other room.

Mr. Moscowitz eyed Robin suspiciously. "Aren't you supposed to be here tomorrow?"

"Bertie, who's at the door?" the woman called again.

Mr. Moscowitz turned around. "It's the adopt-a-child from the school," he announced, "a day early."

"What's that?"

Mr. Moscowitz turned back around and sighed. "She never listens. Married fifty-three years and never once has she listened to me."

A short roly-poly woman with frizzy white hair toddled up. "Where'd you get all these pretty girls, Bertie?"

"They're from the school," he said patiently, "the adopt-a program."

Mrs. Moscowitz looked them over. "We only needed one."

"I *am* one," said Robin. "We were just walking past your house and we wanted to say hello."

Mrs. Moscowitz smiled. "Oh. Now I see. You came to call. How lovely! No one ever comes to call anymore." She turned to her husband. "Bertie, don't let them freeze to death. Invite them inside."

"Okay, okay," said Mr. Moscowitz, throwing open the door. "Come in, girls. Give me your coats." Inside, it felt about ninety-five degrees.

"I'm sure you'll have a little something, won't you?" said Mrs. Moscowitz, disappearing into the kitchen.

Mr. Moscowitz shook his head and turned off the TV. "She'd feed the mailman every day if he let her. Where do you girls live?"

"I live on Washington Street," said Amy. "Have you been here a long time?"

"Fifty years," said Mr. Moscowitz. "We bought this house when Gus was a baby." He pointed to a picture on top of the TV. "That's our Gussie now. He's about to become a grandpa himself."

"Wow," said Erin. "You must be old."

"Seventy-five," said Mr. Moscowitz. "Does that seem old to you?"

Mrs. Moscowitz came back into the living room carrying a tray of cookies and fruit juice.

10

"Here we are, girls," she beamed. "I must tell you. The cookies are dietetic. Mr. Moscowitz has a weight problem."

Mr. Moscowitz snorted. "And she's got the girlish figure."

"What's that?" she said.

"Nothing, dear," said Mr. Moscowitz.

Mrs. Moscowitz passed around some cocktail napkins which read "I'm not old. I'm just not as young as I was." "So," she said, "which one of you will be coming tomorrow?"

"I will," said Robin, who was beginning to look more and more depressed by the minute.

"Do you play bridge?" said Mrs. Moscowitz.

"No," said Robin. She took one bite of her diet cookie and it crumbled all over her lap.

Mrs. Moscowitz smiled. "You will."

"Why?" said Robin.

"Because we're going to teach you!" said Mrs. Moscowitz. "You're going to be Evelyn's partner."

Robin smiled weakly. "Who's Evelyn?"

"My sister," said Mrs. Moscowitz. "We haven't been able to play since her husband, Harry, died last year. She lives next door," she added.

Leah peered out the window. "In the pink house?"

"How did you know?"

"Matching Astro-turf," said Leah dryly.

11

Robin drank a little sip of her warm fruit punch. "Uh, I'm not too great at cards."

"Don't tell Evelyn!" hooted Mr. Moscowitz.

Mrs. Moscowitz leaned over and patted Robin's arm. "Don't worry, dear," she said. "We all have to start somewhere."

"Yes, but . . ."

Mrs. Moscowitz clucked. "Now, now. No complaining. You're going to love Evelyn."

"*Somebody* has to," said Mr. Moscowitz.

"Bertie!" said Mrs. Moscowitz.

Amy stood up. "Uh, I think we'd better get going," she said. Robin gave her a grateful look.

"So soon?" said Mrs. Moscowitz.

"My parents don't like me to be out after dark," said Amy.

"Mine either," said Robin as she scraped her crumbled cookie into her napkin. "I might even have to leave early a few times."

"I'm sure we can work something out," said Mrs. Moscowitz.

Robin was at the door before the others had even finished putting on their coats.

"Good-bye, dear," said Mrs. Moscowitz. "We'll see you tomorrow."

"Okay," said Robin.

The four of them hurried outside.

"I think I'm going to throw up," said Robin.

"Come on," said Amy. "They weren't that bad."

12

"Kind of cute, if you ask me," said Leah. "They remind me of my *bubbeh* and *zayde.*"

"See that?" said Amy.

Robin frowned.

"Maybe you'll learn to like bridge," said Erin.

"Or diet cookies," said Leah.

Robin sighed. "How many weeks is this thing? Four?"

Amy nodded.

"Four long weeks," groaned Robin. "I'm never going to make it!"

Chapter Two

Amy stared at the tiny little heart box sitting on the top of her school desk. Next to it was a slip of paper which said, "To Amy from her secret friend."

"What's that?" said Robin, wandering past. She picked up the little box. "Oooh, how cute. Where'd you get it?"

Amy shook her head. "I don't know. It was sitting here when I got back from lunch. It says it's from my secret friend."

Robin nodded knowingly. "See? I told you someone was interested in you."

Amy glanced around the room. She couldn't imagine who would send her a gift like this, totally unexpectedly.

Robin leaned over and whispered, "Have you noticed any boys staring at you recently?"

Amy's face turned red.

"Have you?" Robin demanded.

"Not really," said Amy.

Just then a few of the boys in her class came in. "What about Brendan Myers?" whispered Robin.

"Robin, stop it!" hissed Amy.

"He's looking over here," said Robin.

"That's because you're acting weird," said Amy.

The bell rang and the students slid into their chairs. *"Buenos dias,* class," said Mr. Hilton, the Spanish teacher. "We're going to start with a videotape today."

Amy took the little box and carefully laid it inside her desk. She glanced slowly to her right. Brendan Myers was studying a comic book stuck inside his Spanish book. Could it be him? Then it happened. Next to Brendan, Grant Taylor, Roddy Casper's best friend, leaned over and smiled at her. A big smile. A big sickening smile.

Amy slammed down her desk top.

"Is something the matter, Ms. Evans?" said Mr. Hilton.

"No," said Amy, gulping.

Just to be sure, she glanced over at Grant again. Another sickening smile. Amy shivered. It was bad enough to have a boy sending you things, but Grant? Yuck! He reminded Amy of a big fat whale with pimples.

Then to make things worse, Amy felt Robin give her a little nudge. When Amy looked over at her, she tilted her head toward Grant and lifted her eyebrows, just to let Amy know she'd seen it all.

Great, thought Amy. Not only does one of the biggest creeps in school like me, but the biggest blabbermouth knows all about it. She couldn't wait to get out of there.

After school, Amy waited for Erin. Today was the day for visiting the adopt-a-grandparents, and Amy and Erin had agreed to walk together. Amy was still thinking about Grant when Erin walked up.

"Why do you look so sad?" asked Erin.

"Sick is more like it," said Amy. "I found out who my secret friend is."

"Who?" said Erin.

Amy made a face. "Grant Taylor."

"Are you sure?" said Erin.

"Positive," said Amy. "He smiled at me during Spanish."

Erin didn't say anything.

"Aren't you at least going to feel sorry for me?" said Amy.

"I guess," said Erin slowly. She looked at Amy again. "Are you *sure* it's Grant?"

"He gave me a little heart box," said Amy. She pulled it out of her jacket.

"That's cute," said Erin.

17

"Do you want it?" said Amy.

"No," said Erin. "He gave it to you."

Amy shrugged and put it back in her pocket. "I guess we'd better get going."

The two girls walked quietly until they reached Polk Street. "Here we are," said Amy, stopping in front of Mrs. Moss' apartment building. Polk Street was on the very edge of Kirkridge in one of the poorer sections of town. The building looked pretty run-down.

Erin gave Amy a pat on the back. "Have fun with Spaghetti Breath."

"Thanks," said Amy. "You have fun with the jogger." She headed toward the front walk. "I'll call you when I get home, okay?"

"Okay," said Erin. "Talk to you later."

Amy let herself into the lobby and walked up two flights of stairs until she found apartment 2C. She was looking forward to meeting Mrs. Moss, even if her breath did smell like spaghetti. Amy knocked on the door and waited. Finally, she heard someone shuffling over.

"Who is it?" said a voice.

"Amy Evans," she answered cheerfully. "From the Adopt-a-Grandparent program."

Amy heard several bolts being unlocked. The door opened a tiny crack and a little old woman about Amy's size peeked out at her.

"Hi," said Amy in her most friendly voice.

The woman looked her over. "Come on in," she said, barely smiling. When she opened the

18

door a little wider, Amy saw that she had white frizzy hair and crooked posture. She was wearing three sweaters over a thin, baggy dress. "This way."

She led Amy into the living room, where she sat back down on an old shabby couch covered with a bedspread. The only other piece of furniture in the room was the TV set, which was directly in front of the couch and looked about a hundred years old. Mrs. Moss motioned for Amy to sit down. Some game show was on TV. Mrs. Moss frowned.

"Would you change that?" she said.

"Sure," said Amy, hopping up. "How's this?"

Mrs. Moss shook her head. Amy changed again. A soap opera.

"That's good," said Mrs. Moss.

Amy sat back down and wrapped her arms around herself, grateful she still had her coat on. No wonder Mrs. Moss had on three sweaters. It was freezing. "How long have you lived here?" asked Amy, trying to make conversation.

"Shhh," said Mrs. Moss, pointing at the TV. At the commercial, Mrs. Moss finally said something. She said, "Go get my coupon basket from the kitchen table."

Amy found the kitchen, found the coupon basket, and returned. Fortunately, the commercial was still on. "My eyes aren't too good,"

19

said Mrs. Moss. "Go through there and throw out the ones that have expired."

"Okay," said Amy, as cheerfully as she could under the circumstances. After she was done with that, Mrs. Moss had her paste in some green stamps and adjust the TV antenna about five times. When the five o'clock news came on, Mrs. Moss said, "When are you coming back?"

"Next week," said Amy.

Mrs. Moss nodded, got up from the sofa, and then walked over and opened the door. "Good-bye."

Amy gave a flimsy wave. "Good-bye," she said.

Back at home, the first thing Amy did was call Erin. "How'd it go, Erin?" she asked.

"Great!" said Erin. "Margaret is so nice."

"Margaret?" said Amy.

"That's what she asked me to call her. You know what we did? We went over to the Children's Museum to check out the new science exhibit. Margaret used to be a children's librarian. She has every book you could imagine in her bookcase. She loaned me her copy of *The Witch of Blackbird Pond.*"

"Nice," said Amy, feeling worse by the minute.

"How was Mrs. Moss? Did you smell her breath?"

"I never got close enough," said Amy. "I was too busy sorting coupons."

"Oh," said Erin. "Not too great, huh?"

"Let me put it this way," said Amy. "Robin doesn't know how good she has it."

"What are you going to do?" said Erin.

Amy was waiting for this question, and she'd already thought it out. "I'm going to stick with it," she said. One thing about Amy, she wasn't a quitter.

Erin gave a sympathetic sigh and then said, "I'm sorry you couldn't get someone like Margaret. She's so neat. She has four children. One of them is an actress and lives in New York. Another one gives guided tours of the Grand Canyon."

"Wow," said Amy. "What about the others?"

"They're just plain."

Amy said, "Next week I'm going to really try to find out more about Mrs. Moss."

"Maybe after she knows you better she'll talk more," said Erin. "Have you spoken to Robin yet?"

"No," said Amy. At that moment, there was a loud pounding on Amy's kitchen door. Amy peered through the curtains and saw Robin staring back at her. "Erin," she said, "Robin's at the door. I've gotta go."

"Okay," said Erin. "See you tomorrow."

Amy let Robin into the kitchen. "Hi," said Amy. "How were the Moscowitzes?"

"Yucky, just like I thought," Robin answered. "We ate diet cookies and tried to play bridge. Only I was terrible at it."

"What was Evelyn like?" asked Amy.

"She looks just like Mrs. Moscowitz only taller," said Robin. She rubbed a spot on her arm. "Every time I did something right, she would pinch me right here and tell me how cute I was. I bet I have a big, ugly bruise tomorrow." She paused. "I wish there were a way I could get out of this."

Amy didn't say anything.

"Oh," said Robin. "I almost forgot. I need to ask you something. Somebody bought the house next to my cousin Matt's and Matt wanted me to ask you if your mom could find out who it is."

"I can try," said Amy. Amy's mother managed a local real estate office.

Just then Amy's mother plowed through the door holding two bags of groceries. "Hi, girls," she said. "Amy, there are more bags in the car, please."

"Okay," said Amy.

Robin stared out the door. "Well, I should probably get home. It's getting pretty dark out there."

"See you tomorrow, then," said Amy. She

hurried outside after Robin to grab some groceries.

The next morning, Amy waited until the last minute so she wouldn't have to see Grant at the bus stop. She timed it so that she would get to the bus just as the last person was getting on.

"Where were you?" Erin asked as Amy walked to the back of the bus and sat down beside her. "I was waiting for you."

"I didn't want to see you-know-who," said Amy under her breath.

Just then Robin leaned forward in her seat. "Your boyfriend was looking for you," she whispered.

"Shhh!" said Amy.

Robin pretended to compose part of her gossip column. "A certain blimp likes A.E.," she said.

Erin turned to Robin. "Stop bothering her," she said angrily. "How would you like it?"

Robin looked crushed. "I'm only teasing," she said.

"Well, stop it," said Erin. "It's not nice to tease."

"Sorry," said Robin. No one said anything for the next few minutes until Robin said, "Did you ask your mom about the house next to Matt's?"

"Oh, I almost forgot," said Amy. "She had

her stuff with her so she looked it up. The owner's name is James Ball. That's all she knows because the house was sold by another realty agency."

Robin nodded and gazed out the window. "Wait a minute," she said, turning suddenly. "Did you say James Ball? Isn't he the guy who plays Bopples the Clown on TV?"

"How should I know?" said Amy.

Robin stood up and at the top of her voice yelled out, "Does anybody know the name of the guy who plays Bopples on TV?"

Roddy Casper stood up in his seat and yelled back, "I do! It's Mr. Eric!"

"Ha, ha. Very funny," said Robin. "I'm serious."

"Why?" said John McCauley, the bus driver. "Looking for a job?"

"Hardly," said Robin. She sat back down with a thump. "I'm sure it's James Ball. I'm going to watch Bopples today and make sure!"

"That'd be sort of neat to have Bopples for a neighbor," said Erin. "The little kids would really like that." Bopples appeared every afternoon on the local TV station. His show had been on forever. His sign-off slogan went like this: "A chuck-a chuck-a chuck-a! Keep on laughing, kids!"

"Have you ever seen him in real life?" asked Robin.

"No," said Amy and Erin together.

"I have," said Robin. "He's a friend of a friend of my dad's. He bought a pair of shoes one time." Robin's family owned Ryan's, the local shoe store.

"What did he look like?" said Amy.

"He had thin gray hair and a potbelly," said Robin. "I had to pretend I didn't know who he was, to protect his identity." She suddenly stopped talking, like an idea had just hit her.

"What is it?" said Amy.

"Nothing," said Robin. "I just thought of something, that's all."

During P.E. that afternoon, Amy had another surprise. When she went to change into her P.E. clothes, there was a note attached to the inside of her locker. "Attention," it said. "Grant Taylor is *not* your secret friend." Signed, "Your Secret Friend."

Amy stared at the note with relief. So it wasn't Grant after all! "What are you looking at?" said her friend Katherine Wolf.

Amy crumpled up the note before Katherine could read it. She wasn't taking any chances having people associate her with Grant. "Nothing," she said. She looked around the locker room for clues. Obviously her secret friend couldn't be a boy because boys weren't allowed in there.

"Hey!" said Robin, popping her head around

the locker. "I heard I was wrong about your secret friend."

"Who told you that?" said Amy suspiciously.

"No one," said Robin, grinning.

"Somebody must have told you or otherwise you wouldn't have known," said Amy.

Robin looked like she was about to spill the beans. "I can't tell," she finally said. "It's a secret."

"Is it a boy or a girl?" said Amy.

Robin grinned a second time. "Sorry, nosey. I said I can't tell. You'll find out soon enough."

"What's that supposed to mean?" said Amy.

But it was too late. Robin had already disappeared around the corner.

Chapter Three

Later that afternoon, Amy, Leah, Erin, and Robin sat clustered together on Amy's parents' king-sized bed, watching TV. As the credits for *Bopples the Clown* started to roll by Robin said, "Now watch, guys."

"There it is!" shrieked Erin. "There's his name. Bopples . . . James Ball!"

"See!" said Robin. "What did I tell you!"

The four girls bounced up and down on the bed. "A chuck-a, chuck-a, chuck-a," they all shouted in unison.

Robin rolled off the bed and sat up on the floor. "Hey!" she said. "If a celebrity is moving to Kirkridge we should do a story, right?"

"Right!" chorused the other three. "A chuck-a, chuck-a, chuck-a."

Just then Patrick stuck his head inside the

door. *"What* is going on, maniacs?" He surveyed the situation and then added, "Amy, Mom and Dad are going to flip out if they see you four toads hopping around on their bed. It's not a trampoline, you know."

"Very funny," said Amy.

"Bopples the Clown is moving to Kirkridge," said Robin. "It's official."

"Yeah?" said Patrick. "I'm thrilled."

"If you were a little kid, you'd be thrilled," said Erin.

Patrick shook his head and walked away.

"What does he know?" said Robin.

Amy bounced off the bed. "Everybody back to the kitchen, please. Time to finish our meeting."

"Can't we stay here?" said Erin. "It's much more fun."

Everyone stared at Amy. "Oh, okay," she said. "As long as we don't eat anything. Mom'll kill me if I spill on the quilt." She grabbed her pencil and notebook off the floor. "Here's what we have so far. The issue is due two weeks from today, okay? Instead of one Neighbor of the Month, we'll have three—Mrs. Moss, Mrs. Donaldson, and the Moscowitzes. Leah will take their pictures next week. What else?"

"Bopples," said Robin.

"That can be your assignment," said Amy. "We'll make it the lead. Find out when he's moving in."

Robin grinned.

"Anything else?"

The others shook their heads.

"How about something for Valentine's Day?" said Erin.

"It'll be over by the time the paper comes out," said Robin.

"I can draw some hearts if you want," said Leah. "Hearts are timeless."

Robin rolled her eyes. You never knew what sort of art Leah was going to come up with.

"That sounds nice, Leah," said Amy. "Can everyone turn in the stories about their grandparents by the end of next week?"

The girls were interrupted by the phone ringing. Amy rolled across the bed to the night table. "Hello?"

A muffled voice asked, "Is this Amy Evans?"

"Yes," she said.

"You have a surprise in your mailbox," said the voice.

"From who?" said Amy.

The caller hung up.

"That was weird," said Amy. "Someone said there's a surprise in my mailbox."

"Let's go see," said Robin, tugging on her shoes.

Inside the mailbox, Amy found a neatly wrapped package with her name on it.

"What is it?" said Leah.

"A new notepad!" said Amy, tearing off the

29

wrapping paper. She opened it up. A card read, "From your secret friend." "Wow," said Amy. "I needed a new notepad. How did my secret friend know?"

"Maybe your secret friend is your mother," said Leah.

Amy laughed. "I doubt it," she said. Unlike the other girls' mothers, Amy's mother was the type who had to be reminded whenever Amy needed something new like shoes or underwear or school supplies.

"Do you have any hints?" asked Erin.

Amy looked at Robin. "No. But Robin knows and she won't tell."

"Robin!" said Erin.

"My lips are sealed," said Robin.

Amy tried to figure out her secret friend's identity. Obviously, it was someone who knew her fairly well. That meant it couldn't be a boy. And she was pretty sure it was somebody from school since she'd already gotten one gift and one message there. Amy looked up the street, hoping to see someone she knew hurrying away, but no such luck.

"Come on, guys," said Robin, heading into the house. "It's freezing out here."

"Okay," said Amy, following her inside. She had to admit, the mystery was starting to get to her.

* * *

By the next week, Amy had received the following things from her secret friend: a little bag of candy hearts with sayings on them, a pencil which said "Happy Valentine's Day," a key chain with a picture of a unicorn, and a copy of a poem called "What is a Friend."

Amy was on her way to study hall on Tuesday when Robin came running up to say, "Guess what! Bopples is moving in the Sunday after next. I'm organizing a welcoming committee."

"You are?" said Amy.

"Welcome to Kirkridge, Bopples," said Robin.

Katherine Wolf and Danielle Stevens came running over. They were both holding their recorders. "Listen to this," said Katherine. They started to play Bopples' theme song.

Robin turned proudly to Amy. "Nice, huh? We're going to try to get a few more."

Amy hesitated. "Uh, Robin. Do you think we're overdoing this? What if Bopples turns out to be the shy type? Maybe this will embarrass him."

"Bopples never gets embarrassed," said Robin.

"But you said one time he came to your shoe store and you had to pretend you didn't know him, to protect his identity."

"This is different," said Robin. "Now he's a

31

resident. Everyone in Kirkridge should know who he is."

"Don't you think a story is enough?" said Amy.

"Hey, Robin," interrupted Brendan, "how big do you want me to make the banner?"

"Banner?" said Amy.

"For Bopples," said Brendan. "He's moving in next week."

"I heard," said Amy.

Erin walked up. "What's going on?" she asked.

"Bopples," said Amy. "Robin's planning a welcoming event."

"Wow," said Erin. She turned back to Amy. "I just remembered something. Isn't Leah supposed to take our pictures today with our grandparents?"

"Oh, right," said Amy. "I hope she remembers."

"Uh, can mine wait?" Robin asked.

"Why?" said Erin.

"Because," said Robin. "I might be switching."

"I thought we weren't allowed to switch," said Erin.

"This would be an exception," said Robin.

Erin stared at her. "Who were you going to switch to?"

"I can't say yet."

32

Erin looked peeved. "You'd better call Leah so she doesn't waste a trip over there."

"Don't worry, I will," said Robin. She waved to someone down the hall. "Hey, Lark. Wait up. I want to ask you something." She turned back to Amy and Erin. "Gotta go. See you later."

" 'Bye," said Amy, watching her disappear.

Erin frowned. "I wonder what she's up to now," she grumbled.

"Who knows?" said Amy. "With Robin, you can never be sure."

Amy sat on the brick wall out in front of the school, waiting for Erin. All week she had tried her best not to think about Mrs. Moss, but the truth was that she was dreading her visit.

"Hi," said Erin. She swung her book bag over her shoulder. "Ready?"

"I guess," said Amy.

"I can't wait to see what Margaret wants to do today," said Erin. "Maybe we'll go for a walk in Forest Park."

Amy tried to imagine Mrs. Moss doing the same thing but she couldn't.

"What are you and Mrs. Moss doing today?" said Erin.

"Probably more coupons," said Amy glumly.

"Don't give up," said Erin. "Remember?"

33

Amy took a deep breath. "You're right," she said. "An Evans never gives up!"

When Amy got to Mrs. Moss's house, Mrs. Moss answered the door wearing her coat.

"Oh," said Amy. "Were you about to leave?"

Mrs. Moss shook her head. "Come on in."

Once again she led Amy over to the sofa and sat down. "There's coupons to sort on the kitchen table," she said.

Amy nodded politely and went in to get the coupons. As she went to pick up the basket, she noticed a cat sleeping on an old green blanket by the stove. "Hi, kitty," she said.

She leaned down to give it a pat.

The cat looked up and purred. It seemed very old.

"Hey, Mrs. Moss," called Amy. "Did you know your stove was on?" She pulled the blanket back a ways so the cat wouldn't burn itself and returned to the living room with the coupon basket.

"What's your cat's name?" asked Amy.

"Gene," said Mrs. Moss. She stared at the TV. "Would you change the channel?"

Amy tried to squeeze in a few more questions. "Why'd you name him Gene?"

"After my brother," said Mrs. Moss. "They both like to sleep. Change the channel, please."

Amy nodded and then asked, "Do you have

34

any children? What happened to your husband? How long have you lived by yourself?"

Mrs. Moss stared at her. "Curious, aren't you?"

"I guess I like people," said Amy. "It's fun to find out about them."

Mrs. Moss said, "I have one son. My husband, Earl, died nine years ago."

"Is your son nearby?"

"He lives in Phoenix. Now would you change the channel?"

Amy flipped to the next channel. "My friends and I have a neighborhood newspaper called the *Treehouse Times*. We wanted to do stories about all of our adopt-a-grandparents this month."

Mrs. Moss looked amused. "There's nothing to tell about me."

"That's not true," said Amy, pulling out her notebook. "I bet you've got lots of interesting things to tell. Where did you live before you came to Kirkridge?"

Mrs. Moss smiled faintly. "On a farm."

"See!" said Amy. "What kind of a farm? Where was it?"

Mrs. Moss got a faraway look in her eyes. "It was in Indiana," she said. "We grew corn."

"I always wanted to visit a real farm," said Amy. "Did you have any cows?"

Mrs. Moss made a face. "Too messy. Earl couldn't stand 'em."

"What about horses or chickens or pigs?" said Amy.

"Only corn," said Mrs. Moss. "Animals are too much work."

"And how did you end up here?"

Mrs. Moss shrugged. "Bad luck," she said. "We lost the farm and Earl thought he could find work in the city."

Amy waited for her to go on but she didn't. "Did he find work?" asked Amy finally.

"Sure," said Mrs. Moss. "But it was never enough."

Amy remembered about Leah. "My friend Leah was going to stop by today to take your picture for our paper. Is that okay?"

Mrs. Moss pulled her coat around herself. "I suppose."

At that moment the door bell rang. "That's probably her," said Amy, hopping up. "I'll get it."

Amy was surprised to see a tall man in a big overcoat standing at the door. "Where's Stella?" he asked.

"Are you her son from Phoenix?"

The man laughed.

"What do you want?" said Mrs. Moss, appearing from inside.

"Your rent check is late," said the man.

Mrs. Moss scowled and turned to Amy. "Wait for me in the kitchen," she told her.

Mrs. Moss stepped outside the apartment and closed the door behind her.

Amy wandered back through the living room and sat down at the kitchen table. She noticed that Gene the cat had scooted back close to the stove, probably to stay warm.

Outside the apartment, Amy could hear Mrs. Moss and the man shouting at each other. She strained her ears. Mrs. Moss said something about the heat. She sounded upset. There was more shouting, this time mostly by the man.

Amy got up from her chair and edged into the living room. The man was carrying on about a mat. Maybe he meant the doormat?

She was just about to sneak a little closer so she could hear better when she saw the door start to open. She hurried back to the kitchen and sat down.

Seconds later, Mrs. Moss rushed in.

"Is everything okay?" asked Amy.

Mrs. Moss bent down and picked Gene up. "There, there," she said, rubbing her face against his ears.

"Who was that man?" said Amy.

Mrs. Moss pursed her lips. "Mr. Delvan."

Amy was just about to ask another question when the door bell rang again. "Now *that's* Leah," said Amy, running to answer the door again. "Good thing," she said, when she saw Leah standing there.

"Why?" said Leah.

"I'll explain later," said Amy. She led Leah into the kitchen. "This is my friend Leah," she told Mrs. Moss. "This is Mrs. Moss and Gene."

Mrs. Moss hardly even smiled.

"Mind if I take your picture?" asked Leah politely.

Mrs. Moss sighed. "If you must." She placed Gene back on his blanket.

"Did you know your stove is on?" asked Amy again.

Mrs. Moss scowled. "Yes."

Leah pulled out a kitchen chair. "Why don't you sit right here?" After Mrs. Moss sat down, Leah carefully moved the plastic placemat and the salt and pepper shakers and pulled up the blinds so that nothing distracted from the picture. "Smile," she said.

Mrs. Moss's mouth turned up a tiny bit.

"Great," said Leah. "A few more."

After Leah was finished, Mrs. Moss said to Amy, "You may as well go. There's been enough excitement for one day."

"But I wanted to ask you some more questions for our newspaper story," said Amy.

Mrs. Moss waved her away. She was obviously in no mood to talk.

"How about if I come back tomorrow?" said Amy.

"I suppose," said Mrs. Moss.

Amy and Leah headed for the door. "I'll be here around four-thirty," said Amy.

"Whatever," said Mrs. Moss. She shut the door behind them.

"A woman of mystery," Leah observed as they climbed down the stairs.

"I'm starting to feel sorry for her," said Amy.

"Why?"

"I don't know. There's something sad about her. I haven't quite figured it out."

They walked quietly for a few minutes.

"Some man came today while I was there. They got into a big fight in the hall."

"What about?" said Leah.

"I'm not sure. I was just starting to ask when you showed up." Amy turned back and looked up at the apartment building. She promised herself that tomorrow she would get to the bottom of this.

Chapter Four

That evening at dinner Amy said, "Mom, do you know a guy named Mr. Delvan?"

Mrs. Evans swallowed her bite of pizza and then said, "Donald Delvan? The landlord?"

"That's him," said Amy. "What do you know about him?"

Mrs. Evans laughed. "Are you planning on moving out?"

"This is serious, Mom," said Amy. "I'm conducting an investigation."

"*Oh,*" said Mrs. Evans, swallowing. She cleared her throat. "Well, he's not a very nice landlord."

"You mean he's a jerk." Patrick butted in.

Amy ignored Patrick and pressed on. "Why?"

Mrs. Evans thought for a minute. "Because

he isn't always fair to his tenants. Does that answer your question?"

"Not really," said Amy. She told her mother about what had happened at Mrs. Moss' that afternoon, how Mr. Delvan had come over and how he and Mrs. Moss had an argument in the hallway.

"What were they arguing about?" said Amy's father, jumping into the conversation.

"I'm not sure," said Amy slowly. "Something about mats, I think."

"*Mats?*" said Patrick.

"No, wait," said Amy. "I also heard Mrs. Moss say something about heat."

"Maybe she wants heated mats," said Patrick.

Amy gave him a stony look. "Very funny."

Amy's mother suddenly said, "Amy, was it very cold in Mrs. Moss' apartment?"

"Freezing," said Amy. "I had to keep my coat on." Her mother looked at her father. "I bet Donald Delvan is withholding heat again. What do you think?"

"Could be," he said.

"Would somebody please explain what you're talking about?" said Amy.

Her mother turned to her patiently. "Landlords are responsible for providing heat for their tenants, which most landlords do without any problem. Sometimes, though, if there is an unethical landlord, he may decide to turn off or withhold a particular building's heat."

"Yeah! Freeze 'em out!" said Patrick.

Mrs. Evans gave Patrick a dirty look. "Patrick, that's enough."

"But why?" said Amy. "What did Mrs. Moss do to deserve this?"

"Who knows?" said Mrs. Evans. "He may be trying to get rid of his tenants because he wants to convert the building to condominiums. Or maybe he just wants to tear the building down."

"That's terrible," said Amy.

"It's also against the law," said her father.

"Why doesn't someone call the cops?" asked Patrick.

Mrs. Evans sighed. "Poor things. Maybe they're all afraid to. That's a small building. He may have already gotten rid of most of the tenants except for a few older people. A lot of elderly people are terrified they'll end up on the street with nowhere to go if they speak up. Men like Donald Delvan prey on them."

"That's stupid," said Patrick. "He's the one breaking the law, not them."

His mother looked at him sternly. "Unless you know the complete circumstances, Patrick, I think you should stop making such rash judgments." She turned to Amy's father. *"Right,* David?"

"Right," he echoed.

43

Amy shook her head. "Poor Mrs. Moss. Maybe the paper can do something to help. Maybe we can write about it."

Mrs. Evans gave Mr. Evans a quick glance and then said, "Amy, I know you're concerned. We all are. But I think this is something you should let *us* handle, not the paper."

Amy was shocked. "Why not?" she asked.

Her mother said, "What if Mr. Delvan finds out that Mrs. Moss is the one who's complaining about him? He can make life miserable for her."

"How?" said Amy.

"Lots of ways," her mother said. "Donald Delvan can be ruthless."

Amy had an idea. "What if we don't mention her name?" she said. "We'll make her an anonymous source like the guy we studied about in our newspaper unit in school. His name was Deep Throat. Did you ever hear of him?"

Amy's father smiled faintly. "Amy," he said firmly, "This is *not* Watergate and you are *not* Deep Throat. Please let us handle this one."

Amy slowly pushed her chair away from the table. "May I please be excused?"

"Where are you going?" said her mother.

In a tight voice she said, "I want to call Erin. Is that allowed?"

"Don't be smart, young lady," said her father.

"Sorry," said Amy under her breath.

"You may be excused," said her mother. "But don't stay on the phone long. You still have homework."

Amy rushed down to the family room, where she knew she'd have privacy. As soon as she got Erin on the phone she said, "I think we have a scoop, but there's a problem."

"What's the problem?" said Erin.

"My parents. They don't want us to get involved. I knew I shouldn't have said anything."

"Well, what's the scoop?" asked Erin.

Amy told her about Mr. Delvan and how he was probably breaking the law. "We have to expose him," said Amy. "We have an obligation to our neighbors."

"Let's do it, then," said Erin.

"We can't," said Amy. "My parents said no. They're afraid Mrs. Moss might get into trouble with Mr. Delvan. I told them we wouldn't mention her name but they didn't like that idea."

"What about freedom of the press?" said Erin.

"I guess it doesn't apply to parents."

"No way," said Erin. "They can't tell us what we can and can't write."

"But they're my *parents*," said Amy. She felt truly confused, especially since she and her

45

parents hardly ever disagreed. Who had the final say?

"When do you see Mrs. Moss again?" said Erin.

"I'm going over tomorrow afternoon to finish my interview," said Amy.

"Then I'm coming with you," said Erin. "We're not even sure Mr. Delvan is doing anything wrong yet, are we? Let's find out what's going on and *then* we can worry."

Listening to Erin, Amy felt better already. "Thanks, Erin," she said. She hung up the phone and flopped back on the sofa. Erin was one of those people you could always count on to calm you down.

Just as she'd promised, Erin went with Amy to Mrs. Moss' the next afternoon. They'd decided not to say anything to Mrs. Moss about the heat until they had a better feel for the situation. As soon as they got there, though, it was obvious things had gotten worse. Besides a coat and several sweaters, Mrs. Moss had on her hat and a pair of furry boots. Amy noticed several blankets piled high on the living room sofa.

"Hi, Mrs. Moss," said Amy. "I'm here to finish our interview."

"Not today," said Mrs. Moss. "I'm not feeling too good."

"But this is my friend Erin," said Amy, pulling Erin forward. "She used to be your paper girl, remember? I told her all about you and about how you lived on a farm your whole life."

Erin nodded. "She did."

"We were really looking forward to this," Amy said.

"Oh, all right," said Mrs. Moss with a loud sigh. "Come on in."

She led them over to the sofa. "Here. Have a blanket."

Amy gave Erin a look.

Mrs. Moss said, "What did you want to ask me?"

Leaving her gloves on, Amy pulled out her notepad, where she'd written down a list of questions. "What did you like about growing up on a farm?"

"That was a long time ago," said Mrs. Moss.

"Did you ever go on a hayride?" said Amy. "I always wanted to go on a hayride."

Mrs. Moss snorted. "That's like asking if I ever rode on a tractor."

Amy's face got a little pink.

"Did you have animals on your farm?" said Erin, coming to the rescue.

"I asked that yesterday, Erin," said Amy.

But Mrs. Moss surprised her by saying, "Not after I got married and Earl and me had our own farm. But when I was a girl I guess we had animals. Sure. Back then everybody had animals.''

"Oh,'' said Amy. "Like what?''

"A goat, a cow, some chickens . . . things we used for food.'' She pulled the blanket closer.

"Did you have any pets?'' asked Amy.

Mrs. Moss thought for a minute. "I had a little pony named Checkers. Used to ride him into town sometimes.''

"Wow,'' said Erin. "You're so lucky.''

Mrs. Moss looked sadly around the room. "Yeah. Sure.''

Amy took this as her cue. "Mrs. Moss,'' she said, "it's awfully cold in here. Did something happen to your heat?''

Mrs. Moss's eyes grew teary. "What heat?'' she said bitterly. "There hasn't been any heat in here for months.''

"Months!'' Amy exclaimed. "You must be freezing!''

"What happened to it?'' said Erin.

Mrs. Moss dabbed at the corner of one eye with her coat sleeve. "Radiator pipe broke last fall,'' she said bitterly. "Mr. Delvan doesn't want to fix it.''

"Why not?'' asked Erin.

Mrs. Moss waved her arm at the wall. "Too cheap. He's got to go in and open up the wall. He'd rather let me freeze to death.''

"But it's against the law to keep heat from

people," said Amy. "Do you want us to tell the police?"

Mrs. Moss turned pale. "No!" she said. "Don't tell the police! Please!"

"Why not?" said Amy. "We don't have to tell him it was you who complained."

Mrs. Moss shook her head. "If he finds out, he'll have me evicted."

"But he can't do that," said Amy. "My mom is a realtor. She said people can't be evicted unless there's a reason."

"I have a reason," said Mrs. Moss. "Gene. I'm not supposed to have a cat." Her eyes got all teary again. "He knows I'd never get rid of Gene. He's all I have."

Amy swallowed. She couldn't believe that anyone could be that cruel to a helpless old lady.

Mrs. Moss straightened herself up and said, "Well, not too much more winter left. Another month or two and it'll be getting warm again."

"But it's supposed to go below zero tonight," said Amy.

"I'll manage," said Mrs. Moss. She poked a long, bony finger at Amy's notepad. "What other questions have you got on there?"

Amy could see that Mrs. Moss wanted to change the subject, but all Amy could think about was mean Mr. Delvan. There had to be *some* way she could get Mrs. Moss' heat fixed without getting her into trouble. She glanced over at Erin, who she could tell was thinking the same thing.

Amy stared at her notepad. "Uh, what was your school like when you were growing up?"

"Now *that's* a good question," said Mrs. Moss, regaining some of her composure. "We had youngsters from all over the county. We carried our lunch to school in tin pails."

As she talked on, Amy tried to listen to what she was saying. Her thoughts, though, were somewhere else. Somewhere a million miles away.

On the way home, Amy and Erin had a lot to talk about. First, there was the problem of what to do about Mrs. Moss. Amy thought that the best thing was to call an emergency meeting as soon as they got back. Leah and Robin needed to know what was going on. And then there was the problem of Amy's parents. Amy didn't even want to think about that one.

As they turned into Amy's driveway, Amy suddenly said, "Hey! I just realized something. It wasn't 'mats'. It was 'cats'!" She went on to explain. "Yesterday in the hall when Mrs. Moss and Mr. Delvan were arguing I heard them talking about the heat and what I thought was 'mats.' Only it wasn't mats. It was *cats*. Now it makes sense."

Amy was surprised to see her mother stick her head out the kitchen door. "Did you forget about your dentist's appointment, young lady?"

Amy stopped in her tracks. Her mother had reminded her yesterday afternoon, but so much had happened since then.

"I've been waiting since four," her mother continued. She didn't look too pleased. "If you hurry, Dr. Kerchoff said he could squeeze you in in about ten minutes."

"But . . ."

"Amy," her mother warned, "don't start."

"Sorry," she mumbled. She turned to Erin. "I guess our meeting will have to be tomorrow. Tell Robin and Leah for me, okay?"

"Okay," said Erin.

Amy slipped into the front seat of the car and sighed. This was one of those times the newspaper would just have to wait.

That night it snowed. As Amy sat in her room working on her homework, all she could think about was poor Mrs. Moss, freezing to death in her apartment. Suddenly she pushed her chair away from her desk and marched down to the family room, where her parents were watching TV.

"Mom, Dad, turn off the TV. I have something to say."

Mr. Evans sat up and immediately clicked off the TV. "Is something wrong, sweetheart?"

"Yes," said Amy. "Mrs. Moss is freezing in

51

her apartment and now it's snowing outside." She went on to tell them what she'd found out and then said, "She doesn't have any friends or family. There's only us."

Mrs. Evans said, "Amy! Why didn't you tell us this before?"

"You told me you didn't want the paper to get involved," said Amy.

"But that doesn't mean *we* can't be involved," said her mother. "Would you like Dad to go check on her?"

"No," said Amy. "I've been thinking it over and I decided that we should rescue her. She and Gene can sleep in my room and I'll stay on the couch."

Silence. Complete silence.

"Mom? Dad?" said Amy.

Mr. Evans cleared his throat. "Uh, Amy. Maybe Mrs. Moss wouldn't be comfortable with that idea."

"Why not?"

"Because," said Amy's mother, "we don't even know her."

"But we're all she has," said Amy. "We can't leave her there. What if she freezes to death?"

There was another long silence. Finally, Amy's mother said quietly, "You're right, Amy. We can't leave her there alone. She deserves to be treated like a human being."

Amy smiled.

"David," said Amy's mother, "maybe you

and Amy can go over there and see if she's willing to come back here."

"Thank you," said Amy.

Her mother reached over and gave her a big hug. "No, Amy. Thank *you.*"

Amy and her father didn't say much on the drive over to Mrs. Moss' apartment. The snow was falling quickly, and hardly anyone was on the streets. They pulled in front of Mrs. Moss' building. "I'm going to let you do the talking, Amy," said her father.

They trudged up the stairs and knocked on Mrs. Moss' door. "Who's there?" she said.

Amy shouted through the door, "It's Amy Evans, Mrs. Moss. I'm with my dad."

Mrs. Moss opened the door. She was still wearing her coat. "Is something the matter?"

"Would you like to come to our house?" blurted Amy.

Mrs. Moss took one step back. "What's that?"

Amy rushed on. "I know how cold it is in here. Would you like to come stay at our house? You can sleep in my room. I'll stay on the couch."

Mrs. Moss looked at Amy's father. "Oh no. I couldn't do that. I don't even know you people."

"It's fine with us, Mrs. Moss," said Amy's father. "We'd be happy to put you up."

"Gene can come, too," Amy chimed in.

Mrs. Moss shook her head. "I don't know. . . . This seems awfully peculiar to me."

"What's peculiar?" said Amy. "It's cold in here. Our house is nice and warm."

Mrs. Moss glanced back at the kitchen. "Well . . ."

"Please?" said Amy. "We'd really like you to come."

Mrs. Moss wrapped her arms around herself and shivered. "Maybe for one night. For Gene's sake. He gets awful chilly."

"Yay!" said Amy.

"I'll get my things," said Mrs. Moss.

Amy grinned at her father. It had been a long time since she'd felt this good.

Chapter Five

The next morning when Amy woke up she could smell pancakes cooking. She rolled off the living room couch and hurried into the kitchen.

"Mom! What are you doing here?"

"I thought Mrs. Moss might like a nice home-cooked breakfast," said her mother cheerfully.

Amy nodded, speechless. The last time she remembered her mother cooking breakfast was when she was in the second grade.

"What's this?" said Amy's father, appearing in the doorway. "Breakfast?"

"Why is everyone so surprised?" said her mother. "We have pancakes occasionally, don't we?"

Patrick slid into one of the kitchen chairs. "Sure, Mom. Once every ten years or so."

"Oh, quit," said his mother, grinning.

At that moment Mrs. Moss walked into the kitchen. Everyone stopped talking.

"Morning," she said.

"Good morning," said Mrs. Evans. "Breakfast's almost ready."

Mrs. Moss smiled politely. "If you don't mind, I'll just have some coffee. I'm not much on breakfast."

Mrs. Evans paused and then said in a perky voice, "Okay."

"Well, *I'll* have pancakes," said Amy.

"Me, too," said Patrick.

Mr. Evans pulled up a chair. "Make that three, honey. It's been a long time since I've had your delicious pancakes. Have a seat, Mrs. Moss. How did you sleep?"

"Pretty good."

"Here's some coffee for you," said Amy's mother. "You sure you won't have any pancakes?" She winked at Patrick. "I only make them once every ten years."

"Oh," said Mrs. Moss, not sure whether or not to laugh. "In that case . . ."

Amy's mother smiled and placed a big stack on the table. "Here. Help yourself. This is a treat for all of us."

Amy was having so much fun at breakfast that she almost missed the school bus. She had to flag John down, and even then she was lucky he saw her.

"Oversleep?" he asked as he swung the bus doors open.

"No, pancakes," she said, hurrying to the back of the bus.

When Robin and Erin saw her, they both started talking at once. "Where were you?" said Erin.

"You never miss the bus," said Robin.

Amy explained how Mrs. Moss was staying in her room.

"Wait a minute," said Robin. "You mean to tell me that Spaghetti Breath is *living* in your room? For how long?"

"I don't know," shrugged Amy. "For as long as she wants, I guess."

"But what if you want some privacy? Where are you supposed to get dressed?"

"I guess in the bathroom like I did this morning," said Amy, starting to get a little bugged.

"Whew," said Robin, shaking her head. "Could you imagine it if Bert and Wanda moved into *my* room? My mother would have a heart attack."

Amy and Erin started to giggle.

"She *would*," said Robin. "She would completely lose it."

"Will you be able to come to our emergency meeting this afternoon?" said Amy.

"Of course," said Robin. "I may have some news of my own."

"What?" said Erin.

But Robin only smiled. "You'll see," she said. "I don't want to say anything until I'm 100 percent sure."

"I'm home," Amy shouted, bursting through the kitchen door. "Anybody here?"

No answer.

Amy ran upstairs to her room. "Mrs. Moss? Are you here?" She noticed that her bed had been neatly made and that all of Mrs. Moss's belongings were gone. The phone rang.

Amy went to her parents' room to answer it. "Hello?"

"It's Mom," said Amy's mother. "How are things?"

"Good. What happened to Mrs. Moss?"

"She asked Dad to drop her off on his way to work."

"Oh," said Amy, feeling disappointed. "Will she be back?"

"I'm not sure," said Mrs. Evans.

Amy was confused. "Doesn't she like it here?" she asked.

"I'm sure she liked it," said her mother. "I just think she may be more comfortable at her house."

"But why?" said Amy. "It's freezing over there."

Mrs. Evans sighed. "I know, Amy. But that's her home. All her things are there."

58

Amy didn't say anything.

"Sweetie, there's something I wanted to mention again," said her mother. "I know that you're concerned about Mrs. Moss, but I don't want your paper tackling Donald Delvan."

It made Amy a little bit mad that her mother was bringing this subject up again, especially since she'd already told Amy how she felt. "Mom," she said, "we just want Mrs. Moss's heat turned back on."

"I know that," said her mother. "We all do." She paused. "I'm going to see if the realty board can't do something right away. He shouldn't be allowed to get away with this."

"Thanks," said Amy reluctantly. She knew the realty board was a lot more powerful than the *Treehouse Times*, but she wasn't sure the board would consider Mrs. Moss's plight as important.

After she hung up the phone, Amy went downstairs to the kitchen to wait for the others. While she waited, she took out a six-pack of diet soda, a bag of chips, and the Valentine's chocolates that her grandmother had sent her this year instead of a check.

Leah banged on the door.

"Coming," said Amy.

Outside, Leah hopped up and down and blew on her hands. "Whew! It's cold!" she said, rushing inside. She sat down at the kitchen table and started to rummage through her bag.

"Here. Happy Valentine's Day." She handed Amy a small package wrapped in tissue paper.

"What's this?" said Amy.

"Something I made," said Leah. "Open it. I have one for Erin and Robin, too."

Amy unwrapped Leah's gift. It was a tiny wire basket. "This is beautiful," said Amy.

"Thanks," said Leah. "It's for candy. I made it with colored paper clips."

Amy managed to squeeze one piece of chocolate into her basket. "Thanks, Leah," she said. "I haven't thought about valentines yet. Too much else going on."

"I know," said Leah. "Erin told me."

Robin and Erin burst through the door. "Brrrr!" said Erin. "I thought my eyelashes were going to freeze shut out there."

While Leah gave the others their Valentine's gifts, Amy got out her notebook. When she was ready, she cleared her throat. "Okay, we're starting," she said.

Robin lowered her voice. "Is she here?"

"No, she went to her house for the day," said Amy.

Robin sat back. "Oh, good. Then we can talk about her."

"The big question," said Amy, "is what we're going to do."

"Why can't she stay *here* for the rest of the winter?" said Robin.

"That's the stupidest thing I ever heard,"

said Erin. "What's Amy supposed to do? Sleep in the living room her whole life?"

"Geez, Louise!" said Robin. "I was just making a suggestion. Don't get so worked up." She plucked two pieces of Valentine's candy from the box and stuck them both into her mouth at once.

"I don't think Mrs. Moss wants to stay here," said Amy diplomatically. "Besides, that doesn't solve the problem."

Everyone sat there for a minute, thinking.

Finally Erin said, "Amy, why can't we do what you said and write the story without mentioning Mrs. Moss's name?"

Amy remembered her mother's warning. "Because if Mrs. Moss gets caught, Mr. Delvan will evict her. We have to be sure she's protected."

Erin said, "Remember that guy we studied in our newspaper unit who was an anonymous source? No one ever found out who *he* was."

"Deep Throat!" said Robin.

"That's where I got the idea," said Amy.

Robin grinned. "He helped those two reporters solve the Floodgate mystery."

"Watergate," said Amy.

"Wait!" said Leah, throwing out her hands. "I have an idea. Why don't we ask Vicky what to do?"

Amy didn't know why she hadn't thought of Vicky sooner. Vicky Lamb was a real reporter and the official advisor for the *Treehouse Times.* She worked for the *St. Louis Post-Dispatch.* "Great!" she told Leah. "Why don't you call and see if she's home?"

While they waited for Leah, Robin and Erin argued about what was in the filling of the dark chocolate squares. Robin said it was cherry, and Erin bet her a dollar it was creamy mint stuff.

From the corner, Leah called over to them, "She's not there. It's her machine. I hate machines."

"Leave her a message," said Amy. "Tell her to call us."

Leah made a face. "I hate these things," she repeated. She swayed from one foot to the other, obviously waiting for the beep. "Call Amy Evans," she said into the receiver. "This is Leah." She slammed down the phone.

"Now what?" said Robin. She bit through half of the chocolate square with her teeth. "One dollar, please, Erin."

Erin scowled.

"Mmmm," said Robin, chewing away. "Delicious. Oh. I almost forgot my announcement."

"What's that?" said Amy.

Robin grinned. "Mr. Eric gave me permission to switch my adopt-a-grandparents."

"Who are you switching to?" said Erin.

"Bopples!" said Robin.

Amy blinked her eyes. "Mr. Eric let you do that?"

"I told him it was good publicity for the program," said Robin.

"But what about Bopples?" said Erin. "What does Bopples say? And who's going to be Evelyn's bridge partner?"

"Relax," said Robin. "I took care of everything. First, so Mr. Eric wouldn't worry, I told him I'd already arranged everything with Bopples."

Amy gasped. "But that's lying! You haven't even met Bopples yet."

"I know," said Robin. "But I'm sure he'll like the idea. I'll take him around and introduce him to everyone."

"But what about Bert and Wanda?" asked Leah.

Robin grinned. "I told Mr. Eric that *you* wanted them."

"*Me?*" said Leah with a squawk. "But I don't even go to your school. Besides, I never said I wanted Bert and Wanda."

"Yes, you did," said Robin. "You said they reminded you of your grandparents, remember?"

"Yes, but . . ."

"Robin," said Erin, "since when do you go around deciding what people should do without asking them first?"

63

Robin stuck out her lip. "Since I didn't think they'd mind."

Amy groaned.

"What's wrong?" said Robin.

"You can't keep doing this, Robin," she told her. "It makes everybody crazy when you do things without telling them."

"But I thought this was a great idea," said Robin.

Leah made a face. "I don't know how to play bridge."

Robin patted Leah's arm. "Don't worry. Neither did I."

Later that afternoon, Amy was still sitting at the kitchen table, working on her homework, when her father got home. "Hi, honey," he said. He came through the door carrying a big box.

"What's that?" Amy asked.

Mr. Evans carefully set the box down on the floor. "Oh, just a little heater I picked up over at the hardware store. I thought since Mrs. Moss was happier at her house, this would help keep her warm."

"That's really nice of you!" said Amy.

"Nah," said her father. He tore open the carton. "Stew Farber has one of these down in his basement. He said it heats up the whole room."

Just then Amy's mother came through the

door, too. "Hi," she said. She eyed the heater. "What's that?"

"A room heater for Mrs. Moss," said Amy's father.

Amy's mother leaned over and gave him a little kiss. "Will you be going over there soon?"

"I thought later," he said.

Mrs. Evans handed him a foil box. "Here. It's barbequed chicken. I got extra for Mrs. Moss." She grinned at Amy. "See what you started?"

"I noticed," said Amy. Inside, she felt all bubbly.

Amy was already in bed that night when her mother knocked on her door and said, "Are you asleep yet?"

"No," she answered, sitting up. She'd been thinking about Mrs. Moss again. When she and her father had taken the stuff over, Mrs. Moss had hardly said a word. She looked pleased, though, like she was glad to have a heater and a warm meal. Afterwards, Amy and her father had talked about it, and her father said that Mrs. Moss was the type who didn't say much.

"Vicky Lamb is on the phone," said Amy's mother.

Amy leapt out of bed. "Oh, good. Thanks, Mom."

"What's up?" said Vicky.

Amy briefly explained the situation and then said, "Can you give us some advice?"

65

"I'd be glad to," said Vicky. "Not right now, though. I'm working on a tight deadline." Amy could hear her thumbing through her appointment book. "Can you come over here tomorrow around six? Sorry it can't be sooner. I've got to be down at City Hall all day covering a trial."

"Uh, I think so. I have to check with Mom."

"Plan to stay for dinner," said Vicky. "I'll order some pizzas, okay?"

"Okay," said Amy.

"Gotta go," said Vicky. "Talk to you tomorrow. Oh, and don't worry. We've got a couple of good options here."

"We do?"

"Yep. 'Bye now."

By the next afternoon, Amy had the whole thing arranged. Everyone was going to meet at Vicky's at six for pizza. Amy was at her locker, getting ready to leave, when she noticed a note taped inside her locker door. "Dear Secret Friend," it said, "Saturday night when it gets dark, be at the swings in Willow Park." Amy looked up. It had been several days since she'd heard from her secret friend. The swings? After dark? At the bottom was a P.S. "Your mom said it was okay."

Amy was curious. What was all this about? Was she going to finally meet her secret friend? And wasn't it sort of spooky, going out

66

after dark? Why would her mother approve? She crumpled the paper up and stuck it inside her pocket. Up ahead, she could see Erin heading for the bus. "Hey, Erin," she called. "Wait up. I want to show you something."

Chapter Six

"Aaah choo!" For the tenth time since they'd arrived at Vicky's, Robin sneezed and wiped her eyes with the back of her hand.

"Are the cats bothering you?" asked Vicky.

"I'll be okay," said Robin. She sneezed three more times.

"The pizza should be here any minute," said Vicky. "Maybe if we were to move to another room . . ."

"No. Really. I'm fine," said Robin.

Erin handed her a tissue. "Here. You're slobbering a little bit."

"I am not!" said Robin, sneezing again.

With a big swoop, Vicky picked up Horace and Wendell from the cushion where they were sleeping. "Okay, guys. Time to move upstairs with Willkie." Willkie was Vicky's other cat. He didn't like people.

Robin blew her nose. "Sorry, Vicky."

"Don't worry about it," Vicky called as she climbed the stairs. "It's time Willkie got to play with something other than dust balls." Upstairs, the cats hissed at one another.

"I didn't know you were allergic, Robin," said Leah.

"Neither did I," said Robin. "I hope I don't have to get shots." She looked around at her friends. "Don't tell my mom about this, okay? She'll have another heart attack." Robin's mother was always worrying.

Vicky came back into the living room. "There!" she said. "Done! Now let's just hope they don't kill each other." From the bedroom came a loud yowl. Vicky grinned. "I didn't hear that, did you?"

"Not a thing," said Leah.

Vicky passed out the paper plates and the soda. "We may as well get started. Tell me the problem again."

Amy explained how Mrs. Moss was afraid to say anything about her heat because she could be evicted because of her cat.

Vicky nodded thoughtfully. "It's hard to believe someone could be so cruel, isn't it?"

Amy said, "We thought maybe the paper could write about her without mentioning her name."

"Like Deep Throat," Robin piped in.

"Only we want to be sure Mrs. Moss is protected," said Amy.

Vicky smiled. "Chances are," she said, "if the landlord is withholding repairs from one person he's doing it to others. If you want, you can do some investigating and see if you can find other tenants who might be willing to go on record. If you can get one of them to talk, then your story will sound more believable."

"And if we can't?" asked Erin.

"Then you can just print your story without naming your source," said Vicky. "Newspapers do it all the time. The story I'm covering right now at City Hall involves an anonymous source."

"It does?" said Robin.

"Sure," said Vicky. "Someone who worked at City Hall came to the paper recently and told us that she'd discovered that one of the officials in the traffic department was taking bribes."

"How did she know?" asked Erin.

"I can't say," said Vicky with a grin. "But anyway, on the basis of what she told us, we did some investigating and sure enough, she was right. So we wrote a story based on the information we'd discovered. We never mentioned our source."

"What happened to the man taking bribes?" Robin asked.

"He's on trial right now," said Vicky. "That's where I've been all day."

"Wow," said Amy. "That's amazing. We just write the story and don't mention Mrs. Moss' name?"

"That's right," said Vicky. "As long as you're certain that you're right. The *problem* with doing it this way is that there's no actual proof. It's just your word against his. In our case, we found proof to back up our statements."

"Won't Mr. Delvan know who we're talking about?" asked Robin.

"Not necessarily," said Vicky. "Like I said, she's probably not alone. Just keep your remarks about her very general. Don't say 'the lady in apartment 4B' or 'the woman on the third floor with the cat.' . . . Get it?"

"I think so," said Amy. She hesitated and then added, "One other thing. My parents don't want us to write about Mr. Delvan."

"Why?" asked Robin. "Do they think he's dangerous?"

"They're afraid he'll find out it's Mrs. Moss and throw her out," said Amy. "They think the paper should stay out of this and that they should handle it."

"But your parents never censored us before," said Robin. She turned to Vicky. "What do *you* think?"

"Good question," said Vicky. "Amy's parents are obviously trying to look after your best interests. Maybe they feel you're not capable of handling this."

"But we are," said Amy. "That's why we came to you for advice before we wrote anything. Besides, this is the perfect chance for the paper to let the public know what Mr. Delvan is doing. If we let my parents fix things then no one will ever find out what a crook he is."

"Spoken like a true reporter," said Vicky, smiling.

"So what do we do?" said Robin.

Vicky sighed. "Obviously, the bottom line here is that a poor little lady is freezing to death and something needs to be done immediately. The question becomes who's going to deal with it? The paper or Amy's parents?"

The door bell rang. "Pizza's here," said Leah.

Vicky stood up and looked straight at Amy. "As editor, the final decision has to be yours, and you need to think very carefully about what you want to do. Maybe you should talk to your parents again and see if you can't convince them that you'll practice responsible journalism."

Amy nodded slowly. "Okay," she said. "I will."

That night after Amy got back from Vicky's, she went to talk to her parents. They were in the family room, watching TV. "I need to ask you something," she said, sitting down on the couch.

"What is it?" said her father.

"Tonight at Vicky's we talked about Mrs. Moss and what the paper could do," she said.

Her mother turned off the TV.

Amy swallowed. "Vicky said if Mr. Delvan is keeping heat from one person he's probably keeping it from others. She said we can write the story in a way that will protect Mrs. Moss. Newspapers do it all the time."

Her mother said, "Honey, before you carry on any further you should know that I spoke with someone at the realty board today. They're sending someone over tomorrow to speak to Mrs. Moss."

"Really?" said Amy.

"Really," said her mother, smiling. "See? I told you we could take care of this without involving the paper."

Amy hesitated and then said, "Uh, Mom, why can't the paper still print its story?"

"They don't need to now," said Mrs. Evans.

"But don't you think Mr. Delvan should be stopped?" said Amy.

Her mother pursed her lips. "Yes. But not by you."

Amy's father interrupted. "Honey, don't you think you're overreacting a little? What's the harm in letting the paper run a story on this guy? What's he going to do? Run over their bikes?''

Amy's mother gave her father a dirty look.

"The paper knows what it's doing, Mom," said Amy.

Her mother shook her head. "Amy, I'm older than you and wiser than you. I would like to think that my judgment on these matters is best.''

"But *why*?" Amy said with a wail. "I don't understand.''

Amy's father leaned over to her mother. "Honey, aren't you being a bit harsh?"

"Oh, honestly, David," said Amy's mother in an exasperated voice. She turned to Amy. "I do not trust Donald Delvan, that's why," she said.

"But that's why the paper should expose him!" said Amy.

"Amy, no," said her mother. "That's final."

Amy folded her arms. "What if we write the story anyway?"

"You'll be grounded for a month," said her mother.

Amy stared at her angrily. "Are you serious?''

"Perfectly serious."

"Then good night," said Amy. She turned on her heel and stalked out.

* * *

Amy thought about her fight with her mother all the next day. The most she'd ever been grounded in her life was a weekend. A long, torturous weekend. She would never be able to survive a month.

Amy tried to remember the last time she'd felt this angry but she couldn't. She was angry that her mother didn't trust her judgment and angry that her mother was telling her what to do. She felt so crummy about the whole thing that all she did all day was lie on the sofa, reading old magazines.

Around five o'clock, Patrick stuck his head into the room.

"What did you do with the blow dryer?" he asked. He was naked except for a big beach towel tied at his waist.

"Nothing," said Amy. "I didn't wash my hair today."

Patrick stared at her. "What's with you? You've been lying here all day."

"So?" said Amy.

"So you never lie around. You're always . . . bouncing."

"Bouncing?"

"You know. Hopping around with your projects."

Amy listlessly lifted one arm. "Mom and I had a fight."

"Is that all?" said Patrick.

"We never fight," said Amy.

"You'll get used to it," said Patrick.

"Ha," said Amy. "You're a big help."

Patrick only shrugged. "How's the old lady?"

"You mean Mrs. Moss? Fine, I guess. I didn't talk to her today."

"Did Mom give you my sleeping bag?" Patrick asked.

"She's still at work," said Amy.

"It's for Mrs. Moss," said Patrick. "It stays warm to fifteen below."

Amy looked at her brother in amazement. "Patrick! You're letting Mrs. Moss use your down sleeping bag? You won't even let *Dad* use your sleeping bag."

Patrick grunted. "It's only a loan. I want it back, understand?"

"That's really nice of you," said Amy.

Patrick waved her off. "Maybe Mom took the hair dryer into her room," he said, disappearing.

"Maybe," said Amy. She glanced out the window again and then suddenly jumped up. Her secret friend! She was supposed to meet her secret friend at the swings in Willow Park when it got dark. She'd been so preoccupied that she'd forgotten all about it. She put on her parka, hat, and gloves and hurried outside. Maybe her friend was still there.

Willow Park was a tiny little patch of green over near Lincoln Avenue. Calling it a park was really more of a joke than anything. The only thing parklike about it was an old broken down swing set.

Amy picked her way through some broken beer bottles over to the swing set. Empty. Not a person in sight. Amy sat down to wait. It was creepy here. Cold, dark, and creepy.

On the frozen ground a flapping white envelope caught her eye. "For Amy," it said. She reached down and picked it up. "Go to Aegean Pizza and ask Mr. P for your order," it said.

"My order?" said Amy. "I didn't make any order."

She stuck the note in her pocket and hurried around the corner, glad for an excuse to leave the park. "Ahhh, Miss Pulitzer!" said Mr. Petropoulus as she came through the door. "You here for your order?" "Miss Pulitzer" was Mr. P's nickname for Amy. He was a good friend of the newspaper.

"I guess," said Amy, starting to feel very confused.

Mr. Petropoulus handed her a pizza with a message scrawled across the top of the box. "Go to the Sugar Bowl."

"Did you write that?" Amy asked.

"Sure!" said Mr. Petropoulus in his booming voice. "But I'm not going to tell you who told me to." He laughed out loud.

Amy tried to smile but she was in no mood for a joke tonight.

"Go on, young lady," he said. "Kay is expecting you."

Amy scuffed down the block. "Hi, Kay," she said, shoving open the door.

"There you are!" said Kay. She handed Amy a bag.

"What's this?"

"Banana splits made with chocolate chip ice cream and butterscotch and marshmallow sauce."

Amy rolled her eyes. "For *me?*" Her secret friend must really like to eat. Maybe it was Robin.

"For you," said Kay. She handed Amy another note.

"Go to the treehouse," read Amy. "Or else." She looked at Kay. "But it's freezing out!"

"Hey," said Kay, "I'm only following orders."

Amy trudged off. She was starting to get curious again. What was the next surprise waiting for her?

From the front yard of her house, Amy could see someone moving around inside the treehouse. She cautiously approached the ladder and called up, "Anyone home?"

Someone stamped three times on the floor. Thump, thump, thump.

Amy swallowed. "I'm coming up," she said. Balancing the pizza in one hand and the banana splits in the other, she slowly climbed the ladder.

Amy pushed open the hatch and adjusted her eyes to the darkness. Someone had hung millions of twinkling little Christmas lights around the room. A Melody Rollins tape was playing.

"Surprise!"

Erin, Leah, and Robin leapt out from behind the sofa.

"Eeeek," screamed Amy, almost dropping the pizza. "What are you doing here?"

"It's a Valentine's treehouse pizza party," said Erin. "Get it?"

"But what about my secret friend?" said Amy.

"I'm your secret friend," said Erin.

Amy's mouth opened. "You?"

Erin flashed a smile. "Fooled you, didn't I?" She took the pizza and banana splits out of Amy's arms. "Have a seat, please."

Amy peered around at all the flashing lights. "It looks beautiful in here," she said.

"Thanks," said Erin. "We stretched an extension cord from your kitchen. That's why you had to leave your house."

"Notice the heater?" asked Robin. "Nice and toasty."

"But why are you guys doing this?" Amy asked.

"Why not?" said Erin. "I got the idea for a secret friend from camp."

"But none of the notes was in your handwriting," said Amy. "And what about that phone call?"

"That was Danielle," said Erin, grinning. "And I had all different people write the notes and deliver them so you wouldn't suspect me."

Amy was touched. "All the little presents?" she asked. "And the reporter's notebook and the box I thought Grant—ugh—had given to me?"

Erin smiled modestly.

"No wonder my secret friend gave me such good stuff. It was you!"

"Hey," said Robin. "Enough of this mushy stuff. I'm hungry."

Amy started to giggle. "Whoever heard of a pizza party in a treehouse in February?"

Erin tore off a big slice of pepperoni-mushroom. "To my secret friend," she said, "Happy Valentine's Day!"

Amy bit into the slice. "Happy Valentine's Day," she said with her mouth full. It felt great to be in a good mood again.

Chapter Seven

Amy was blasted out of bed the next morning by Patrick who was yelling into her ear, "Phone call for Amy Evans. Phone call for Amy Evans!"

Amy groaned and fumbled for her glasses. She looked at her alarm clock. "Seven forty-five," she mumbled. She opened one eye and stared at Patrick. "What are you doing here? You never get up this early on Sunday morning."

"I'm not up," said Patrick. "I had to answer the phone."

Amy rubbed her eyes. "What happened to Mom and Dad? Why didn't they answer?"

"They're not here. They went to the Sugar Bowl for breakfast."

"Without us?" said Amy.

Patrick started to jump on the end of Amy's bed. "Up, up, up."

Amy felt herself getting smashed against the wall. "Ow, stop it, Patrick. Who is it, anyway?"

"It's Robin," said Patrick. "Something about Bopples."

Amy sat up. "Oh, wow. I almost forgot. Today's the day Bopples moves in." She rolled off the bed. "Thanks, Patrick."

"No problem," he said. "I love being woken up at this hour. First by Mom. Now by you."

Amy went into her parents' bedroom and stretched herself out on the bed. "What's up?" she said, yawning into the phone.

"Bopples' furniture is here!" said Robin.

"Where are you?" asked Amy.

"I'm at Matt's house. I spent the night in Adrienne's room, remember? Today is our welcoming party." Adrienne was Matt's baby sister.

"Oh, right," said Amy, trying to wake up.

"Bopples has some nice furniture," said Robin. "A *huge* stereo system with *huge* speakers. About eight TVs."

"*Eight TV's?* Are you sure?"

"Maybe more like five," said Robin. She paused. "Three for sure. When are you coming over?"

Amy pulled her parents' quilt up around her chin. "I told you. I can't come until after Sunday school and then lunch. It'll be at least two o'clock."

"But the welcoming party starts at two. Can't you be here a little earlier? I need help with the food."

"Food?" said Amy. "What kind of food?"

"I got stuff Bopples will like . . . popcorn, jelly beans, soda."

"Oh," said Amy. "Okay. I guess I can do that." She heard her parents downstairs. "I'll see you later, okay?"

"Hi there," said her father, walking into the bedroom.

"Hi," said Amy. "How was breakfast?"

"Yummy," said her mother. She squeezed Amy's father's hand. "We haven't done that in years, have we, sweetie?"

"Centuries," he said.

Amy's mother sat down beside her on the bed. "Speaking of centuries, I feel like it's been that long since I've seen you."

"It has," said Amy. Even though almost two days had passed since their fight, she was still feeling funny about everything.

Her mother smiled. "How did your party go in the treehouse?"

"Fun."

"Were you surprised?"

"Yes."

Her mother waited. "And????"

"And what?"

85

"Tell me about it," said her mother. "What did you do? Who was there?"

"Erin, Robin, and Leah," said Amy. "We danced to tapes and ate cheezies dipped in hot sauce."

"Sounds like fun," said her mother.

Amy crawled out from under the covers.

"Where are you going?"

"I thought I'd check on Mrs. Moss before Sunday school," said Amy.

"That's a nice idea," said her mother. "Find out whether they were able to do anything about her heat."

Amy nodded. "I'll meet you at church."

Mrs. Moss was doing her laundry in the kitchen sink when Amy arrived. "Why don't you take that to the laundromat?" she asked.

"Too much trouble," said Mrs. Moss, scrubbing away. Amy noticed that Mrs. Moss still had the little heater her father had brought running full blast in her bedroom.

"Where's Gene today?"

Mrs. Moss pointed to her bedroom. "Where do you think?"

Amy watched Mrs. Moss wring out her things and hang them in the bathroom to dry.

"A man stopped by from some realty place yesterday," said Mrs. Moss. "Do you know anything about that?"

"I think my mom sent him," said Amy.

"He thinks he can get my radiator going."

"That's great!" said Amy.

Mrs. Moss smiled. "You tell your mother I appreciate this."

Amy slowly ran her finger along the tub. "What would you think if our newspaper did a story about Mr. Delvan not giving you heat? We wouldn't mention your name so that Mr. Delvan wouldn't be able to prove it was you."

Mrs. Moss didn't say anything.

Amy said, "I don't think Mr. Delvan should be allowed to get away with this, do you?"

Mrs. Moss dried her hands on a towel and then looked Amy right in the eye. "I don't want any trouble, see?"

Amy nodded, even though she didn't see at all. How could there be trouble if they didn't mention her name? Why was everybody so paranoid? Feeling disappointed, she went into the living room to find her coat.

"Where are you going?" called Mrs. Moss.

"Sunday school," said Amy.

"Are you coming back?"

"Not today," said Amy. "I'll be back Tuesday."

Mrs. Moss came into the living room. "Then here," she said, handing her a card. "Happy Valentine."

That's the way she said it, Happy Valentine, without the s.

"Thanks," said Amy, smiling. It made her feel much better knowing Mrs. Moss liked her enough to buy her a card. Amy opened it up. It was one of those old-fashioned cards with the swirly flowers and hearts on it. She had signed it, Fondly, Stella Moss.

"That's pretty," said Amy. "I mailed yours yesterday. You should get it tomorrow."

Mrs. Moss nodded.

"Well," said Amy. " 'Bye. Have a happy Valentine's Day." She impulsively leaned over and gave Mrs. Moss a little hug. Even with all her sweaters, Mrs. Moss felt as thin as a first grader.

"You too," said Mrs. Moss, patting her arm.

Funny, thought Amy. All the time she'd known Mrs. Moss she'd never noticed how frail she was.

Robin dumped a large bag of red jelly beans into one of her Aunt Dinah's wicker baskets. "What do you think?" she asked Amy. "Should we mix in the candy kisses or should they be separate?"

"Uh, mixed, I guess," said Amy.

Robin nodded and stuffed a few more jelly beans into her mouth. Amy wasn't counting, but Robin must have eaten at least half a bag by now.

"Ooops," said Robin, "almost forgot the popcorn." On the kitchen counter, the O'Connor's popcorn popper was popping away. They already had six bowls, but Robin wanted one more to add bubblegum flavoring to.

The door bell rang. "I'll get it," yelled Robin, grabbing a few chocolate kisses as she headed for the door.

In the front hall, Amy could hear some kids saying, "A chuck-a, chuck-a, chuck-a!" It sounded like Brendan Myers with Matt O'Connor.

"Aaamy," yelled Robin. "Come see this banner."

Amy turned off the popper and went to see. "Wow," she said, walking into the hall. The banner must have been fifteen feet long. "Welcome to Kirkridge, Bopples," it said. Brendan had drawn a clown in one corner and some circus animals in the other. "It's beautiful."

"Thanks," said Brendan.

Other kids started arriving, crowding into the hall. "Has anybody seen him yet?" asked Chelsea Dale, pushing her way inside.

"Not yet," said Robin.

Chelsea got this satisfied look on her face and said, "Well I just saw a car pull up and a man carrying some books and stuff got out."

"That's him," screamed Robin. "It's Bopples!"

The three kids who were supposed to play their recorders started tooting away. "How soon do we leave?" asked Katherine Wolf.

"A few more minutes," said Robin. "Leah and Erin still aren't here." There was some more confusion.

"Don't anyone rip the banner," yelled Robin. She grabbed Amy's arm. "The food. Help me with the food."

"Robin, calm down," whispered Amy.

"I can't. Bopples is next door," she said. She barreled into the kitchen again.

Finally, Erin and Leah arrived. "Sorry," said Leah. "I forgot my camera and had to go all the way back home."

Erin laughed louder than usual and said, "Not too smart, Leah."

Leah rolled her eyes at Amy. For months now, Erin had a crush on Matt O'Connor, and it was a known fact that whenever Matt was in the vicinity, Erin wasn't herself.

Robin came back carrying three bowls of popcorn. "Attention, please," she shouted. "We are leaving here in five minutes." Matt tried to take a handful of popcorn but Robin slapped his hand. "No touching the merchandise."

"It's my house," said Matt.

"It's my popcorn," said Robin. They both cracked up, causing Erin to laugh hysterically.

"Line up, everyone," said Robin. She passed out the bowls of popcorn and candy to people she thought wouldn't snitch them and then said, "Now here's what we're going to do. As soon as Bopples answers the door, we'll all say 'Welcome, Bopples. A chuck-a chuck-a chuck-a.' Does everyone have that?"

"That sounds stupid," said Matt.

"It does not," said Robin. "Is everyone ready?"

"Ready!" they all shouted.

Robin raised her arm. "Let's go, then!"

The welcoming party carefully made its way across the O'Connor's front lawn and over to Bopples' house. Robin spent a few minutes getting the banner opened up and the musicians in place. "Okay," she finally said. "I'll ring the bell."

Ding, dong.

A young guy wearing jeans and an oversized sweater answered the door. Amy thought it might be Bopples' son, but before Robin could say anything, the rest of the kids yelled, "Welcome, Bopples. A chuck-a chuck-a chuck-a," and the musicians started in playing their recorders.

"Stop," yelled Robin. "Not yet. Wait, guys."

Everything ground to a halt.

"Is Bopples here?" Robin asked the man politely.

The guy laughed. "What is this?" he said. "Some kind of joke?"

"We'd like to see Bopples," said Robin firmly.

The man stared, first at the banner and then at all the kids. "Who?"

"Bopples. James Ball." Robin looked like she was starting to get a little annoyed. "He's supposed to be moving into this house today."

The man started to laugh. Slowly, at first, but then louder and louder, until pretty soon he was holding his stomach he was laughing so hard.

"What's so funny?" said Robin indignantly.

"*I'm* James Ball," he said. "James Avery Ball." He wiped a tear from the corner of his eye. "Listen, kids, I appreciate the reception, but I have to tell you that I don't know who this Bopples character is."

Robin's face was turning the color of her hair. "But James Ball plays Bopples the Clown on TV," she said.

"Not this James Ball," said the man, cracking up again. "The only thing I play is the guitar."

"But . . ." Robin looked mortified.

Erin slid over to her and whispered, "Didn't you check?"

"*You* were watching the same TV I was," Robin hissed.

"Uh, listen, kids," said Mr. Ball. "It looks like you went to a lot of trouble for this Bopples. He must be a great guy."

"He is," said Robin, desperately trying to

save her reputation. "Are you sure you're not related to him?"

The man laughed again. "There are a lot of clowns in my family, but no one named Bopples."

Chelsea wrung her hands. "Now what do we do?" she said.

Robin quickly pulled herself together. "We re-group," she said. "We go back to the O'Connors' house and eat up the food we made." She smiled nicely at James Ball. "You're invited."

"Uh, thanks," he said. "I think I'll pass."

The welcoming party hurried back across the O'Connor's front lawn. "This is *so* embarrassing," said Erin under her breath.

"Tell me about it," said Leah. "The only good thing is that I don't get stuck with the Moscowitzes."

As soon as they were back inside Matt's house, everyone jumped on Robin. "You should have checked to make sure it was the right James Ball," said Erin, pointing an accusing finger.

"How was I supposed to know there were two?" she said. "Quit blaming me."

"But someone should have checked," said Katherine. "How come no one thought about this?"

"Good point," said Amy.

Robin turned to Amy. "Yeah! You're the editor," she said. *"You* should have thought of this."

"I'm not the one who told the whole school," said Amy.

"So?" said Robin. "That's not my problem. You should have stopped me." She grabbed one of the popcorn bowls. "I'm hungry," she said, marching into the family room. "Let's eat."

"Yeah," said Brendan, following her inside. "Enough fighting. Let's eat."

Later that afternoon, Amy and Erin were sloshing their way home along Washington Street.

"What a great party," said Erin, probably thinking about Matt and the one time he spoke to her all day which was to say, "Hey, Valdez, quit hogging the popcorn."

Amy didn't answer.

"Is something the matter?" asked Erin.

"Yes," said Amy. "I've been thinking about what Robin said."

"Forget about Robin," said Erin, brushing her off. "She never takes the blame for anything."

"I know," said Amy, "but it got me thinking."

Erin stared at her. "What are you talking about?" she said.

"I'm talking about the paper," said Amy.

94

"Today when Robin blamed me for Bopples, even though I know she always blames everyone else, I realized something. I realized that I can take this person's advice or that person's advice, but it's *my* guilty conscience I have to live with if I don't do a good job."

"What's that supposed to mean?" said Erin.

"It means I think the public has a right to know just what a slimeball Mr. Delvan is. It means that if I don't, then I have to live with my guilty conscience."

"Amy," said Erin, "are you telling me that you're willing to be grounded for a whole month just to save your guilty conscience? Are you sure this is what you want to do?"

"Positive," said Amy. "It's worth the sacrifice." She tapped her fingers against her glasses, the way she always did when she was thinking. "You'll have to distribute the paper without me, and you'll probably have to organize the next issue, too. Think you can do it?"

"Sure," said Erin, grinning. "But we'll miss you."

They reached Amy's driveway. Amy gazed up at the front door.

"Want me to come with you when you tell your parents?" asked Erin.

"Not necessary," said Amy, suddenly feeling very good about her decision. "I can do this one myself."

Chapter Eight

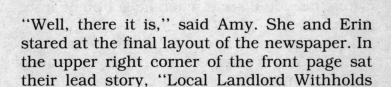

"Well, there it is," said Amy. She and Erin stared at the final layout of the newspaper. In the upper right corner of the front page sat their lead story, "Local Landlord Withholds Heat."

Amy read the opening paragraph out loud one final time. "Local landlord Donald P. Delvan is being accused of withholding heat from one of his tenants. The tenant, who lives in Mr. Delvan's building at 4223 Polk Street, says that her apartment was without heat for most of the winter." Amy looked up. "Do you think that gives too much away about Mrs. Moss' identity?"

Erin shook her head. "Nope. It could be anyone."

Amy nodded and quickly leafed through the

rest of the issue, which looked pretty skimpy. As Erin had suggested, they didn't include the profile on Mrs. Moss this issue since people might be able to figure out that she was the one who didn't have heat. Without the story about Bopples and without the profile on Mrs. Moss, Leah had had to draw a lot of cupids instead. The cupids were Leah's idea. There were cupids dancing, cupids painting, cupids playing cards, and cupids on roller skates.

Amy carefully put the layout into a large manila envelope, wrote "Dad" on the front, and left the envelope on the kitchen table where he would see it when he got home from work.

In a deep, slow voice, Erin said, "The deed is done. Amy Evans, you are hereby grounded for one month."

"Don't remind me," said Amy, wincing.

"Sorry," said Erin. "I was trying to be funny but I guess I wasn't so funny."

Amy smiled weakly. Thinking about it made her feel bad all over again.

"How about one last banana split at Kay's?" said Erin. She dug into her jeans pocket and pulled out a couple of crumpled dollar bills. "My treat."

"Okay," said Amy, grinning bravely. "May as well make the most out of my last day of freedom."

* * *

Amy's grounding started that weekend. All day Saturday, Amy felt like she was in a time warp. It wasn't that she missed watching TV or talking on the phone. She was never big on those things anyway. What was driving her crazy was not being able to talk to her friends and check up on the paper. Did it get distributed? How did it go? What did people think?

Determined to keep herself busy, Amy started in on a huge stack of books she'd checked out of the library. She also began to re-organize her closet. Skirts and dresses on the left side, blouses on the right, sweaters on top. Not that she had that many clothes. It was more something to do to keep her mind off things.

By Monday, Amy couldn't wait to see her friends. When she got to the bus stop, everyone ran up and crowded around her.

"Amy, we missed you!" said Erin, giving her a hug.

"How did it go?" asked Amy anxiously.

"No sweat," said Robin.

"All the newspapers were delivered on schedule," said Erin.

Chelsea piped in, "I helped."

"Any word about Mr. Delvan?" asked Amy.

"Nothing yet," said Erin. "Robin and I ran into Vicky on Saturday. She told us that because of our article, the health department will

99

probably investigate the complaint. If Mr. Delvan is guilty, he'll be fined a lot of money."

"Five hundred dollars for every day of no heat," said Robin. "Or ninety days in jail."

"Wow," said Amy. She'd had no idea Mr. Delvan could go to jail.

"What about Mrs. Moss' heat?" Robin asked. "Was it fixed?"

"Mom said they were able to patch it up without tearing down the wall," said Amy.

"Then it was all worth it," said Erin. "Mr. Delvan got in trouble and Mrs. Moss got her heat."

Amy smiled. "Right," she said. "It was all worth it."

That afternoon, Amy was busy working on her closet when the phone rang. She thought Patrick was home, but after the phone rang about eight times, she decided she'd better get it herself, even though she wasn't supposed to be talking to friends on the phone.

"Hello?" she said.

A voice growled, "I'd like to talk to Amy Evans."

"Speaking," she said.

"This is Donald Delvan," said the voice.

Amy gulped. "Yes?"

"Young lady," he said, "I received a phone call from the city health department this morning. They read me an article which they said you wrote."

"Yes?" said Amy again. Her heart had started to pound.

"Your newspaper has made some pretty serious charges against me," said Mr. Delvan.

Amy swallowed. "I know."

"Well I'd like to know where you got your information," he said. "You can't go around making irresponsible accusations like this, you know."

"They're not irresponsible," said Amy. "They're true."

"Can't be," said Mr. Delvan. "All of my tenants have heat. Ask any one of 'em."

"I did," said Amy. "My information is correct."

"Listen here," he said harshly, "this isn't some school assignment we're talking about."

Amy started to get angry. "I stand by my story," she said in a firm voice. "You have been withholding heat from one of your tenants all winter."

Mr. Delvan sighed. "Okay, kid," he said. "You want to play ball in the big leagues? You want to stand by your story?"

"Yes," said Amy, not as bravely this time.

"Then prove it!" said Mr. Delvan. "It's your word against mine, young lady. If you want your story to stand, you'd better be able to name some names."

Amy pursed her lips. "I'm sorry, Mr. Delvan, but I can't reveal my source."

Mr. Delvan laughed. "Then in that case," he said, "I demand a retraction. Do you know what that means?"

Before Amy could tell him, Mr. Delvan cut her off. "It means you publicly apologize to me in your next issue for making untrue and slanderous statements."

"And what if we don't?" asked Amy, her heart beating a mile a minute.

"I'll sue you for libel," he said calmly. "You're smearing my good reputation."

"But I'm telling the truth," said Amy. "Besides, I'm only eleven years old."

"Then I'll sue all your parents," he said. "Not only that, I'll get the court to serve a permanent injunction against your newspaper so it can't be printed ever again. How would you like that?"

Amy felt as if the room had just come crashing down on her head. "You can't," she said helplessly. "You can't take away our paper."

"Oh, no?" said Mr. Delvan. "Try me."

"Wait," said Amy desperately. "Don't hang up. I need some time to think about this."

"I haven't got any time," said Mr. Delvan. "The health department's breathing down my back."

"Give me a few days to think about it," Amy begged.

Mr. Delvan growled. "Okay. I'll give you until Wednesday night to either issue a retraction or tell me where you got your information. Understand?"

"Understand," said Amy. Mr. Delvan slammed down the phone.

Amy sat down on her parents' bed. Her hands wouldn't stop shaking.

"Anybody home?" called Patrick downstairs.

The pressure was too much. Amy burst into tears.

"What's wrong?" said Patrick, coming into the bedroom.

Amy tearfully spilled out the whole story. "What am I going to do?" she sobbed. "I don't want to tell on Mrs. Moss but I don't want Mom and Dad to be sued."

Patrick shook his head. "He's got you coming and going." He stared at Amy. "You *sure* you don't want to print a retraction?"

"Never!" said Amy.

"Think about it," said Patrick. "You wouldn't have to spill Mrs. Moss' name and Mom and Dad wouldn't have to be sued."

"But then Mr. Delvan would win," said Amy.

"So?" said Patrick. "Mrs. Moss' heat is already back on, isn't it? What's the big deal?"

"The big deal is that if he gets off this time, what's to keep him from doing the same thing next year and the next and the next?" said

Amy, the tears welling up all over again. "Mrs. Moss is still a victim."

Patrick sat quietly for a minute. "I see what you mean." He gave a sideways look at Amy. "Your glasses are fogging up."

Amy sniffled and took them off to dry.

From downstairs, a voice called. "Yoo-hoo."

Amy froze. "Mom!" she whispered. "I don't want her to see I've been crying."

Patrick calmly hopped off the bed. "Hi, Mom," he said, strolling into the hall.

"Where's Amy?" she asked.

"Organizing her closet," said Patrick, bounding down the stairs. "Hey, I want to show you the new exhaust pipe I put on my bike!"

"Is it noisy?" asked their mother. "I don't want any more noise around here."

"Naw," said Patrick. "Quiet as can be. Here. I'll show you." They walked into the garage.

Amy slowly got up from her parents' bed and made her way back into her room. She was glad to have some time to think. Everything was such a mess.

For a long time, Amy sat very still underneath her hanging clothes, trying to pretend that nothing had happened. She hoped that if she sat there long enough, the whole thing would turn out to be a dream.

Amy heard her mother's voice. "Amy? Are you in here?"

Amy pressed herself back against the wall.

"Amy? Is that you?"

"Not exactly," Amy said.

She could feel her mother rustling through the hangers. "Where are you?"

"Down here," said Amy glumly. "Between my plaid skirt and my navy jumper."

Her mother's green eyes peered down at her. "Are you feeling all right?"

"I guess," said Amy. She curled herself into a little ball. "Mom, if you don't mind," she said, "I need some privacy."

"Sure you don't want to talk?" said her mother.

"Positive," said Amy. "I have a lot of thinking to do before tomorrow."

By the next morning, Amy had come up with a plan. On the way to school, she told Robin and Erin what had happened.

"Wait a minute," said Robin, when she heard the news. "Let me get this straight. Mr. Delvan is going to sue *my* parents? For money?"

"That's what he said," Amy answered. "He's going to sue all of our parents."

Robin groaned. "I *knew* we shouldn't run this story," she said. "Knowing my mom, she'll take it out of my allowance." She shook her head. "She'll probably make me sell all my

105

possessions, too. My TV. My canopy bed. My clothes—"

"Robin," interrupted Erin, "what about the rest of us? We're in just as much trouble as you are. And what about the paper? What if he shuts down the paper?"

"There's only one solution that I can see," said Amy, "and for it to work we have to move fast. We only have until tomorrow."

"I'm ready," said Erin eagerly.

Amy continued. "We have to come up with some proof that Mr. Delvan has been withholding heat."

"In other words," said Erin, "we have to find someone willing to go on record, right? That's what Vicky said at that meeting we had with her."

"Right," said Amy.

"How are we going to do that?" said Robin.

Amy looked at them both. "You have to go to Mrs. Moss' building and start knocking on doors. See if anyone else has had problems and wants to say something."

"But today is Tuesday," said Erin. "We have adopt-a-grandparents."

"Don't remind me," said Robin.

"You can go afterwards," said Amy.

"And what if nobody says anything?" asked Robin.

Amy sighed. "If they don't, we lose the paper and our parents get sued. Simple as that."

* * *

That afternoon when Mrs. Moss met Amy at her door, she was only wearing one sweater.

"Toasty in here," said Amy.

"It's been toasty for a couple days now," said Mrs. Moss. She looked right at Amy. "I hope you don't get yourself in trouble on account of all this."

Amy laughed nervously. "No way," she said. "What kind of trouble could there be? I'm only eleven."

For the rest of the afternoon and evening, Amy could barely keep her mind on anything. She wished she weren't grounded. She wished she could be with Robin, Erin, and Leah as they went through Mrs. Moss' building. Were they having any luck? Was anyone willing to talk?

Around seven-thirty, Amy was working at her desk when she heard a snowball hit her window. She looked outside and saw Erin hopping up and down.

Amy quickly opened the window. "Did you do it?" she called down in a whisper. "Did you find someone?"

"It didn't work," said Erin. "We must have asked every person in the building. They all said they had plenty of heat."

Amy's shoulders dropped.

"Amy!" said Erin. "We can't give up yet. Re-

107

member what you said? An Evans never gives up.''

"But . . ." Amy didn't know what to do next. She was all out of ideas.

"Doesn't Mr. Delvan own other buildings?" asked Erin.

"Yes, but where?" said Amy.

"Find out," said Erin. "Get your mom to tell you and we can ask them tomorrow. We still have one more day left."

Amy took a deep breath.

"Come on," said Erin. "You don't want to lose the paper, do you?"

Amy heard her mother's voice. "Amy, who are you talking to in there?"

Amy leaned out the window. "Gotta go," she whispered quickly. "I'll give you the information tomorrow."

Amy barely had the window shut when her mother knocked on her door.

"Come in," said Amy, throwing herself onto the bed.

"Were you talking to someone in here?" said her mother.

"Uh, I was practicing my lines for a play we're doing in history tomorrow," said Amy.

"That's nice," said her mother, sitting down on the bed. She wrapped her arms around herself. "It's chilly in here."

"I had the window open to let in some fresh air," said Amy.

108

"Amy," said her mother, "I hope we can be friends again after all this. I'm sure you understand that when I asked you not to publish the story about Mr. Delvan I only had your best interests at heart."

"I know," said Amy.

"And I hope you understand that I had no choice but to ground you when you deliberately disobeyed me," her mother went on. She shook her head. "I must say, you've been handling it very well. I'm surprised no one has heard from Donald Delvan."

Amy cleared her throat to keep from choking. "Has he been a landlord for a long time?" she asked.

"Fairly long," said her mother. "His father owned a number of buildings around town which he inherited."

Amy's heart started pounding again. "Besides Mrs. Moss' building, what other ones does he own?"

"Oh, I don't know," said her mother. "He owns that old firetrap over on McKinley. And he owns a bunch of buildings downtown."

"Which firetrap?" said Amy.

"That red brick building on the corner of McKinley and Taft that looks like it's falling down."

"Oh, right," said Amy. "Anything else? I mean, does he own any other buildings in Kirkridge."

"That's it, thank goodness," said her mother.

"Thank goodness," echoed Amy, falling back onto her pillow.

"This is our last chance," Amy told Erin and Robin the next morning. "You *have* to find somebody in this building."

"We'll try," said Robin.

"You've gotta do more than that, Robin," said Amy, feeling the desperation start to creep up her neck.

"Don't worry," Erin said. "We'll do it. We promise we will."

"Remember," said Amy. "I'll be waiting for you guys outside our garage at five-thirty."

At five-thirty on the nose, Amy threw on her parka.

"Where do you think you're going?" asked Patrick.

"Uh, I just want to see what the weather's like," said Amy.

Patrick gave her a knowing look. "Right."

Under her breath Amy said, "If Mom comes downstairs, cover for me, okay? I'll be back in a minute." She hurried on outside.

"Well?" she said, rushing to the other side of the garage where Leah, Erin, and Robin were huddled. She took one look at Erin's face and immediately knew what had happened.

"I'm sorry, Amy," blurted Erin.

"You failed?" said Amy, disbelieving.

"We really tried," said Leah. "We knocked on every single door in that building."

"Cross our hearts and hope to die," said Robin. "They're all scared of Mr. Delvan."

"I'm beginning to know how they feel," Amy mumbled. She turned and headed inside.

"Wait," said Erin. "Where are you going?"

"I think I'd better tell Mom the bad news before Mr. Delvan calls," she said.

Amy dragged herself through the kitchen door. Her mother and Patrick were standing by the dishwasher. "Where have you been?" she asked.

"Mom, I have something to tell you."

Patrick cut in, "I told her you thought you left something in the car."

"Never mind, Patrick," she told him. "Mom, I have something to tell you," she repeated. "Yesterday I got a call from—"

They were interrupted by the phone ringing.

"Excuse me, Amy," said her mother, answering it. "Hello?"

Amy winced. It was Mr. Delvan. It had to be. Now she wasn't even going to get a chance to tell her mother first.

"It's for you," said her mother, handing her the receiver.

"Oh," said Amy, surprised. "Hello?"

"My name is Clare Kozloski," said the

111

woman. "I sometimes play cards with Wanda Moscowitz."

Amy had to think for a minute. "You mean Wanda of Bert and Wanda?"

"That's right," said the woman. "That's how I got your phone number. I saw that you wrote a story in your newspaper about them so I figured you must know them."

"That's right," said Amy, wondering where the conversation was going.

"I also read the story about Mr. Delvan," she said. She clucked her tongue. "A very bad man."

"Do you know him?" asked Amy.

"He's my landlord," she said. "Not only that, today your friends came around to my building, wanting to know if I had any problems with my heat."

"And . . . ?" said Amy.

"And they seemed like such nice girls," said Mrs. Kozloski. "So sincere. So after they left I called Wanda. She told me how Mr. Delvan is about to sue your parents."

Robin and her big mouth, thought Amy.

Mrs. Kozloski continued. "You know something? That man has been threatening me for years, just like he's probably doing to that other woman. Can you imagine that? What a crook."

"Mrs. Kozloski," said Amy slowly, "are you willing to let our paper print your name?"

112

"I figure," she said, "that if a bunch of young girls are willing to tackle Donald Delvan, why shouldn't an old lady? Besides, I'm moving in with my sister next month."

If Mrs. Kozloski had been in the room, Amy would have given her a big kiss. Instead, she kissed the nearest person in the room, who happened to be Patrick.

"Hey! Knock it off!" he said.

"I can't help it," she answered. "The paper has just been saved!"

Chapter Nine

After Amy hung up the phone, she had a lot of explaining to do. Needless to say, her mother was upset when she heard about Mr. Delvan. "Amy!" she said in a shocked voice. "Why didn't you tell me about this sooner!"

"I thought you'd be mad," said Amy.

Her mother slowly shook her head. "I just can't believe that Donald Delvan would actually try to sue us. What a creep." She gave Amy a hug. "You must have been very frightened."

"I was," Amy said.

That night when Mr. Delvan called back, Amy was waiting for his call in the kitchen.

"Donald Delvan here," he said. "You got something to tell me?"

Amy could barely control her excitement. "That's right," she answered. "Do you have a tenant named Mrs. Kozloski?"

"What about her?" said Mr. Delvan.

In a clear voice Amy said, "According to Mrs. Kozloski, you've been withholding heat from her all winter."

"That's a lie," said Mr. Delvan.. "She doesn't know what she's talking about."

Amy held her ground. "She can prove it," she insisted. "She said she's not afraid of you anymore. She's moving in with her sister."

Mr. Delvan muttered a few bad words.

"Mr. Delvan?"

"Listen, kid, why don't you learn to mind your own business?"

Amy's mother, who had been listening in, grabbed the phone from Amy and said, "Don't you talk to my daughter that way!"

"Mom!" hissed Amy.

But Amy's mother was on a roll. "I can't believe that a grown man, a man who should know better, would even *think* about terrorizing innocent children and old people," she yelled. "Donald Delvan, you're not fit to call yourself a landlord. I hope they strip your license this time and send you to jail for as long as they possibly can!"

Amy grabbed the phone back from her mother. "Me, too!" she said. "I hope they send you to Siberia!'' She slammed down the phone and took a deep breath.

"Siberia?" said her mother. She started to laugh, which made Amy laugh, too.

Amy laughed until she thought her sides were going to split open. Then she started to cry. She guessed that it was because all that pressure finally had somewhere to go.

On Saturday morning when Amy woke up, she could smell pancakes cooking again. "What's the matter?" she asked, walking into the kitchen. "Why are we having pancakes?"

Her mother smiled. "New policy."

"What do you mean?" asked Amy.

"I thought it would be nice to start a family tradition. Pancakes every Saturday morning. Besides, we should celebrate. Thanks to you, Donald Delvan is in big trouble!" She held up Thursday evening's edition of the real paper, the St. Louis Post-Dispatch, and pointed to the headline: SLUMLORD DONALD DELVAN IN HOT WATER.

Amy giggled. "Maybe he'll go to Siberia after all."

Her mother laughed back. "I'm serious, Amy. If it weren't for you, the Post-Dispatch wouldn't have picked up the story and all those other tenants wouldn't have come forward."

Amy smiled modestly. Things couldn't have

worked out better if she'd planned it. After the real paper had interviewed her and run its own story, three more people had gone to the Health Department with complaints about Mr. Delvan. Vicky said he'd probably have to go to jail.

Amy's mother flipped the pancakes and then said, "In view of all that's happened in the last few days, I've been thinking about your being grounded. A month may have been a bit harsh. I've decided to commute your sentence. As of today, you're a free woman."

Amy couldn't believe it. "I'm free?" she said. "No more grounding?"

Her mother gave her a hug. "No more grounding. I think we've all learned some lessons. Promise me one thing, though," she said. "From now on, you'll listen to your mother's wisdom a little better."

Amy thought about what her mother said and all that had happened. Then, very carefully choosing her words, she answered, "Okay, Mom. I'll try my best."

Announcing the new debut of America's favorite stories from beloved author, Beverly Cleary!

MEET THE GIRLS FROM CABIN SIX IN

Coming Soon

CAMP SUNNYSIDE FRIENDS #5
LOOKING FOR TROUBLE

75909-8 ($2.50 US/$2.95 Can)

When the older girls at camp ask Erin to join them in some slightly-against-the-rules escapades, she has to choose between appearing cool and being mature.

*Don't Miss These Other
Camp Sunnyside Adventures:*

(#4) NEW GIRL IN CABIN SIX

75703-6 ($2.50 US/$2.95 Can)

(#3) COLOR WAR! 75702-8 ($2.50 US/$2.95 Can)

(#2) CABIN SIX PLAYS CUPID

75701-X ($2.50 US/$2.95 Can)

(#1) NO BOYS ALLOWED! 75700-1 ($2.50 US/$2.95 Can)

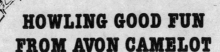

HOWLING GOOD FUN
FROM AVON CAMELOT

Meet the 5th graders of P.S. 13—
the craziest, creepiest kids ever!

M IS FOR MONSTER

            75423-1/$2.75 US/$3.25 CAN

by Mel Gilden; illustrated by John Pierard

BORN TO HOWL   **75425-8/$2.50 US/$3.25 CAN**

by Mel Gilden; illustrated by John Pierard

THERE'S A BATWING IN MY
     LUNCHBOX   **75426-6/$2.75 US/$3.25 CAN**

by Ann Hodgman; illustrated by John Pierard

THE PET OF FRANKENSTEIN

          75185-2/$2.50 US/$2.50 US/$3.25 CAN

by Mel Gilden; illustrated by John Pierard

Z IS FOR ZOMBIE   **75686-2/$2.75 US/$3.25 CAN**

by Mel Gilden; illustrated by John Pierard

MONSTER MASHERS

            75785-0/$2.75 US/$3.25 CAN

by Mel Gilden; illustrated by John Pierard